FERNGULLY

FERNGULLY

Diana Young

SCHOLASTIC INC.
New York Toronto London Auckland Sydney

Printed on recycled paper.

Illustrations by Jean Maxine Perramon.
Cover art:
  Art direction: Matt Perry
  Design: David Stewart
  Character line art: Bill Morrison
  Character painting: Pam Easter
  Background: Dennis Venizelos

Previously published in Australia in 1992 by Ashton Scholastic Pty. Ltd.

ISBN 0-590-45433-1

12 11 10 9 8 7 6 5   2 3 4 5 6 7/9

Printed in the U.S.A.   28

First Scholastic printing, April 1992

*For Bindo, Tui and Nuro, and for
children everywhere.*

*A special thanks to Jim Cox for his
enormous contribution to this story,
and to my sons Scott, Stuart
and Nik, who added their own brand
of humour to FernGully.*

CONTENTS

FernGully

Deep in the heart of
every forest
there is a place which is
greener and quieter
than anywhere else.
In this rainforest, that
place is called
FernGully.

1

THE FOREST WAKES UP

As the first light of dawn crept into FernGully, Crysta woke up. This was the time of day the tiny fairy loved best. She swung out of her cobweb hammock, careful not to wake her two sisters, and tiptoed out of her sleeping hollow. She fluttered up the spiral staircase inside the trunk of the towering strangler fig tree where she lived, and opened a tiny fungus door. But when she stepped onto the branch outside, she discovered she wasn't the only one awake.

A flock of rainbow lorikeets darted through the trees. Suddenly the forest was alive with bird calls, as the dawn chorus erupted into a short, vibrant song.

Crysta fluttered her turquoise wings and dived out of the tree, into a delicate blanket of mist. She fell past a million sparkling dew drops, somersaulted through the mist then, just before she hit the ground, pulled out of her dive and spiralled upwards. She danced in the air to the beat of the birds' early morning song, then practised a few loop-the-loops and barrel rolls.

'Watch out, Lorry!' she shouted, colliding with a rainbow lorikeet. The lorikeet squawked and darted after her.

'You don't own this forest, Crysta!'

'Oh, bug off, Lorry!' She laughed, catching hold of a trailing pepper vine and swinging on it through the trees.

'I can out-fly you any day,' Lorry squawked.

She grinned. 'That's a laugh! You fly about as fast as a wet brush turkey.'

'Then let's see who gets to Palm Grove first,' he chirped, darting through the trees ahead of her.

Crysta accepted the challenge and flew after him. Speed flying was her favourite sport, and she knew she was one of the fastest flyers in the forest. Only her elf friend, Pips, came close to beating her.

She easily caught up to the lorikeet, matching him turn for turn as they dived over the tops of tree ferns and walking-stick palms and zig-zagged around the trunks of huge red cedar and brush box trees.

They crossed the creek at Python Rock and darted through Sleepy Hollow. Crysta waved to Stoneface as she streaked past.

'I'll bring you back something special,' she shouted to her favourite rock, wondering if he ever really heard her.

She chased the lorikeet around tangled vines and prickly ash. They twisted and turned through Fallen Tree Gap. They soared way up to the treetops, turning just below the canopy, then hurtling back to earth and skimming across the forest floor. A noisy pitta bird screeched and ducked for cover as they buzzed dangerously low overhead.

Both of them knew that flying at this speed was forbidden by fairylore. But neither of them slowed down.

The lorikeet knew he was finally beaten when Crysta shot past him in a dazzling burst of iridescent blue light.

'That's a fairy trick!' he complained, flapping into the branches of a tall flame tree, where he disappeared among the bright red flowers.

She laughed. 'Come on, Lorry! I *am* a fairy.'

But the lorikeet refused to continue the race on the grounds that, being a fairy, she had an unfair advantage. Crysta didn't bother to argue with him and continued flying.

By now the forest was bathed in dappled morning light, and she was ready to join in the buzzing morning activity. Dancing playfully across shafts of sunlight, she helped a bee collect honey, then stopped to watch a flock of rowdy parrots squabble over ripe fruit. A wompoo pigeon cooed 'Good morning', and she joined in a song with the frogs.

Everywhere she looked, the forest was busy: a fussy brush turkey scratched in the soil to build a high dirt mound for his nest; worried green ants searched for food, and wanderer butterflies flitted gracefully between flowering blueberry ash and native wisteria.

She followed a narrow path through the trees, humming an old fairy song and stopping every now and again to collect spider webbing and tiny seeds. These she tucked carefully into her cobweb pouch, the magic pouch old Magi Lune had given her many summers ago.

Crysta smiled as she thought about Magi Lune.

Magi Lune was the oldest fairy in the forest, so old that Crysta's grandfather used to say she'd been there since the very first tree.

Crysta felt excited when she remembered the old fairy's promise to her.

'Some day I will teach you the Old Powers, for knowledge must never be lost. But first you must grow up!'

'When will I *ever* grow up?' Crysta wondered, jumping onto a shaft of sunlight streaming through the canopy of the forest. Sliding down it to the forest floor, she landed with a bump on a wet leaf and skidded across it, crashing into a heap of leaves rotting beneath an umbrella tree.

'Who's there? Who's there?' snuffled a familiar voice from a nearby burrow.

'It's me, Crysta. Only I'm covered in mulch!'

A long-nosed potoroo slowly hopped out of his burrow, looking more like a mouse than anything else—except his nose was much longer. The potoroo was very old. He was almost blind, and in some places his fur didn't quite cover the bald spots.

Crysta smiled at him while she dusted herself off. 'Hello, Potsy, I haven't seen you for ages. Where have you been?'

The potoroo sat up on his hind legs, clasping his tiny front paws. His whiskers bristled nervously as he sniffed the air.

'Oh, hello, Crysta. I haven't seen anyone,' he said.

'No, I said where have you *been*!'

'No need to shout!' he sniffed. 'I've been down at Thunder Falls. But it's too damp for me down there. You stay away from those falls. The frogs are getting all worked up.'

4

'What about?' she asked, gently stroking his long whiskers.

'They're talking about the old tales,' he replied mysteriously.

'What old tales? Do you mean *human-tales*?' Crysta fluttered into the air with excitement.

'No,' he sniffed, glancing over his shoulder to see if anyone was listening. 'And you come back down to earth. Don't go filling that pretty head of yours with human-tales.' He twitched his whiskers nervously. 'No, the talk was about the weather, and why it's not the same as it used to be. Everyone at the falls thinks someone is playing around with it.'

Crysta was amazed. 'But that's weather-working! That's straight out of fairy legend.'

'Well, the weather *is* all topsy-turvy,' he snuffled. 'You don't have to be a frog to notice that.' And then he whispered, 'Everyone thinks the weather is being worked by Hexxus.'

'Hexxus?' spluttered Crysta, goggle-eyed. 'Wasn't Hexxus an evil spirit who tried to destroy this forest a long time ago?'

The potoroo nodded. 'That's the one. But what worries me is why anyone is remembering Hexxus at all. Those old tales are best forgotten, they just stir everyone up and that always means trouble. But nevertheless, there is an unnatural force in this forest at the moment, I can feel it in my bones.'

'Don't worry, Potsy,' said Crysta, feeling sorry for the nervous old potoroo. 'There's nothing in this forest to hurt us, you know that. I'm sure there's a good reason why the weather's a bit scatty. I'm not scared of frog talk.'

'Just be careful all the same,' he said, nodding his

worried little head.

'And you take care of yourself,' replied Crysta. 'I wish you'd come back to *Old Hi Rise*, where I could look after you.'

'I can look after myself,' he snuffled. 'But it's kind of you to offer.'

As she fluttered away from the old potoroo, she thought about what he'd said. 'Weather-working,' she muttered, startling a bright orange butterfly. 'What if someone really is working the weather? Do you think it is possible?'

The butterfly didn't reply.

'Don't you worry, I'll ask Magi Lune, she'll know,' Crysta said to the butterfly.

But the butterfly still didn't reply. It wasn't worried about a thing. On this sun-drenched peaceful morning, it didn't have a care in the world.

A long-nosed potoroo slowly hopped out of his burrow, looking more like a mouse than anything else— except his nose was much longer.

2
MAGI LUNE

Crysta sped back towards Python Rock. Long shafts of golden sunlight now streaked the forest, and she realised she'd wandered a long way from home.

'It's later than I thought,' she muttered to herself. 'Now I *am* in trouble! I've missed dance class again. Rose Myrtle will be furious.'

But she didn't go home. Instead, she crossed the creek at Python Rock, turned left at Fossil Bend and headed into a mist-shrouded Antarctic beech tree forest.

Crysta loved this corner of the forest, for she knew it was bursting with ancient secrets. Like Magi Lune, the trees that grew here were very old. Most of them were decorated with long, trailing fingers of soft lichen which shimmered a ghostly green in the hazy light.

After flying for a while, she came to the oldest stand

of Antarctic beech trees. In front of them slept two enormous cassowaries. They were Ock and Rock, Magi Lune's minders. When they heard Crysta, they unwound their long necks from under their wings and opened their bleary eyes.

'Who goes there? Friend or foe? Answer quick or out you go,' mumbled Rock.

'State your name, Crysta,' said Ock importantly.

'*And* the password,' added Rock. 'Please, Crys! We hardly ever get a chance to use the password.'

'All right—*isginitz*,' she said, saying the first word she could think of.

'Is that the password?' asked Rock.

'Sounds fine to me,' nodded Ock, scratching the bone on top of his head.

'See you later,' called Crysta.

'*See you later*... Could that be it?' asked Ock.

''Bye,' said Crysta.

'*'Bye*—that's it!' he shouted.

'You dumb bonehead!' groaned Rock, '*'bye* is not the password.'

'Don't call me a bonehead, you great big useless lump of feathers!' squawked Ock.

While the two birds quarrelled, Crysta slipped past them, stepping over a carpet of golden leaves to enter the inner circle of trees. Light streamed through arched openings which were filled with sparkling, dew-covered spider webs and delicate butterfly wings, creating a kaleidoscope of soft colours.

The entrance to Magi Lune's house lay behind a cluster of delicate tree orchids. Crysta tugged on a well-worn vine that hung beside the moss-covered door. While she waited for the door to open, she smoothed her crumpled leotard and ran her fingers through her dark unruly hair. She hoped Magi wasn't asleep, but it was always hard to tell. The old fairy kept different hours to everyone else. She lived her life by the phases of the Moon. Crysta wondered if this was the reason the fairies and elves of FernGully thought she was crazy.

The door swung open and Crysta peered inside. In one corner of the darkened hollow Magi sat, on a roughly carved stool in front of a cluttered bench. Her long petalled robes hung to the floor, covering her feet.

A glow-worm lantern flickered faint light over an unfurled parchment scroll. Crysta saw that Magi was staring into a tiny diamond-shaped crystal.

'Hello, sweet-wings,' Magi said, without taking her eyes off the crystal. 'You got here faster than I expected. Come closer, I want you to look into this crystal and tell me what you see.'

Crysta fluttered over to Magi, but when she looked into the crystal it was cloudy—she couldn't see a thing.

'That's what I'm worried about,' sighed the old fairy, fossicking through the pockets of her robe. Finding a strand of spider webbing, she twisted it between her thin fingers and tied back her mop of wild hair to stop it falling in her eyes.

'I've sat up day and night, trying to understand what this means,' she said. 'For the first time in my life, the future is unclear.'

'Magi, the frogs think Hexxus is back in this forest and working the weather,' Crysta whispered. 'Could it be true?'

'Hexxus?' spluttered Magi, knocking over a basket of green river stones as she turned to face Crysta.

9

'And just what do you know about Hexxus?'

Crysta frowned. 'Not much. Except what I remember from the fairy legends and what old Potsy told me.'

Magi looked at Crysta thoughtfully. 'Some things are best forgotten,' she muttered, floating away from the bench and flopping into a soft feather chair. Crysta followed her and sat on a low mushroom stool by her feet.

When Magi finally spoke, her voice sounded different, as if she was travelling back in time, to some long-forgotten place.

'Crysta, remember how I've told you that within us all is the power to create or destroy? Well, the story of Hexxus is a story of destruction.'

The old fairy closed her eyes, and was silent for a moment. When she spoke again, she sounded tired, as though the memory of Hexxus weighed heavily on her mind.

'You see, Crysta, Hexxus was the spirit of destruction. You could even say he was born to destroy. His part in the web of life was to get rid of the old to make way for the new. But as Hexxus grew, he realised what incredible power he held. And he knew, that if he wanted to, he could use that power to end *all* life.

'And so he introduced fear into a world that knew no fear. From that day on Hexxus turned into the most dangerous and evil monster the world has ever known. He worked the weather and brewed up unnatural storms. He could change his shape and size, and become whatever he wanted to be, and this made him almost impossible to recognise. He began to kill life as fast as it grew, upsetting the very balance of nature. He had to be stopped before he destroyed us all.'

'Oh Magi, was it *you* who stopped him?' asked Crysta, wide-eyed. 'Did you work the Old Powers?'

Magi nodded. 'I was young then. Hexxus and I had a terrible battle. The forest was ripped apart. Too many lives were lost.'

Her hooded eyes glistened with tears and her voice dropped to a whisper. 'Yes, in the end I *did* defeat Hexxus. You see Crysta, the love I felt for this forest gave me a power Hexxus knew nothing about. And nothing he threw at me could weaken that power. The stronger I got, the weaker he became, until he was just a dark, wispy shadow. I eventually trapped him in the roots of a huge old tree at the foot of Mount Warning. The mountain and the trees have guarded him day and night ever since.'

Crysta stared at Magi Lune. 'Could he ever escape?' she whispered fearfully.

'No! There isn't a force in nature that could release Hexxus now,' Magi replied firmly. 'No, the trouble I feel at present is different.'

Magi Lune pulled herself out of her chair and floated outside. Crysta followed close behind her.

'Crysta, I think the time has come to begin the teaching I promised. We must try to turn your curiosity into knowledge!'

Trailing behind her, Crysta watched the forest respond to Magi's presence. Flowers opened as she passed, and butterflies fluttered around her. Birds began to sing, and even the moss turned greener when she floated by. Crysta wished that she could float in the air without using her wings.

Magi chuckled, reading her mind. 'There's more to

magic than floating,' she said. Next, she defied gravity by rising vertically into the air.

'You know how to do all these things, you've just forgotten,' she told Crysta. 'Once upon a time, there wasn't a fairy alive who didn't know all the magic there was to know. The trouble is, when life gets too easy there's not the same need for magic, so it gets forgotten along the way.'

But no matter how hard she tried, Crysta couldn't float in the air without using her wings. In fact, she couldn't do most of the things Magi asked her to do. She couldn't invisible herself, and she couldn't even perform the simplest changing spell.

Finally, Magi showed her the plants she used for healing, and when the lesson was over Crysta realised how little she knew about anything. But Magi told her not to lose heart. 'You'll find your own way if you practise,' she assured her. 'Remember, there is little I can teach you that you don't already know, but once you care for others, your magic powers will grow.'

Excited, Crysta left Magi Lune's house eager to get home. But she didn't go far before she ran into trouble.

3
SKYLARKING

Crysta was so busy thinking about Hexxus that she didn't notice a huge spider web strung between the trees, and she flew straight into it.

The web was the work of a golden orb weaver, a big yellow and black striped spider.

'Sometimes you miss what's right under your nose, and that can be dangerous,' said the spider. 'Hmmm, fairy, no less! Must be my lucky day.'

'Oh, no!' cried Crysta, desperately trying to disentangle herself from the web.

'I like *fairy*,' said the spider, creeping menacingly towards her.

'You stay away from me!' Crysta warned. 'Don't you dare eat me. You wouldn't like me anyway. I'm all wings.'

'Are you kidding? I love wings! Nice and crunchy.'

'Well, if you don't let me go, I'll cast a spell and

change you into a...a gecko!'

'Pooff,' said the spider. 'The only thing you can change, my dear, is your attitude. What are you doing out here?'

Crysta told the spider she was checking out whether or not Hexxus really was working the weather.

'Spin the silk and stretch the webbing!' the spider said, its eight eyes almost popping out of its head. 'And what are you going to do about it? A skinny little thing like you couldn't do much.'

'I'm a fairy, and I can do all sorts of magic things,' said Crysta, hoping she sounded convincing. But the spider didn't believe her, and asked Crysta to prove she was magic. So Crysta closed her eyes, held out her arms and concentrated.

The flash of red that suddenly appeared next to the web surprised her almost as much as the spider.

'Pips!' she cried, as an elfin-faced boy unfolded his amber wings and hovered in the air beside her, grinning.

'I've been following you,' he said, 'and I must say you've been flying like an old mothball. Fancy flying into the oldest trap in the world, fly-face! Lucky I was watching out for you.'

'I could have managed on my own!'

'That's a load of turkey-mould and you know it!' He laughed and helped her out of the web.

'Hello, Pips,' said the spider. 'Pity you turned up. I was having fun.'

'Fun!' spluttered Crysta. 'It may be *your* idea of fun, but you were about to eat me.'

'Nah,' replied the spider. 'I never eat fairy. No taste.'

'Then why did you have to frighten me to death?'

14

'You were so busy jumping to conclusions, I didn't have to say much. But take my advice, Crysta, and practise up on your magic. You could need it. Remember, your boyfriend may not be around to help you next time.'

'He's *not* my boyfriend!' Crysta blushed, then laughed, as she waved goodbye.

Relieved to be out of the spider's web, Crysta fluttered quietly through the trees. Flying backwards beside her, Pips played his flute. They took a short cut through the forest and crossed the creek at Deadwood. Suddenly the atmosphere changed. The air now smelt heavy with rotting leaves. Pips tucked his flute under his arm and turned around.

'There's something following us. I know there is,' Crysta said, looking back over her shoulder as they picked their way through thickly-woven vines.

'Only your shadow!'

She took his hand. 'Pips, do you remember any of the old forest legends?' she asked.

'You mean the stories about goblins and trolls and evil spirits? Come on, Crys, aren't you a bit old for fairy legend?'

'But what if those stories are true?' she insisted.

Pips just laughed at her. 'Hey, don't get your wings in a twist!' he said. 'There are no evil spirits, you featherbrain. They don't exist.'

'I'm serious about this, Pips. There's something weird going on in this forest, and I'm going to get to the bottom of it.'

'And I think you've been listening to too much frog talk. Word has it that you've been spending so much time with Magi Lune lately, you've gone seedy.'

'Is that so? Then watch this!' she said, letting go of

his hand and disappearing through the tangle of vines, leaving her trail of iridescent blue behind her.

Just then the sound of the Beetle Boys kick-starting their noisy staghorn beetles pierced the quiet of the forest.

'We've got you covered this time,' yelled Stump, their leader. 'And ya gonna be mulched!'

'Have to catch us first!' shouted Pips, streaking after Crysta.

The race was on. It was a race with absolutely no rules. The Beetle Boys didn't believe in rules, in fact they didn't believe in anything outside their noisy beetle world. They were fast-living, fast-flying elves who'd become so attached to their beetles they'd almost become part of them. No-one knew where they'd come from, but just about everyone agreed they were a dirty, no-good lot who weren't welcome in FernGully.

Four of them now chased after Crysta and Pips as they flew as fast as they could towards Thunder Falls. Pips knew how much the Beetle Boys hated water, so he figured they'd never follow them up the raging waterfall.

Soaring and plummeting, twisting and spiralling, Crysta and Pips raced through the forest. The Beetle Boys followed close behind, weaving their way through webs of vines then streaking along the glassy surface of the creek, narrowly missing low branches (and terrifying baby Platts and mother platypus who were enjoying a quiet swim).

But no matter how fast and noisy they were, the Beetle Boys were unable to manoeuvre their beetles to match the dazzling display of speed flying by Crysta and Pips.

At the foot of the waterfall, Crysta shot up through the spray, narrowly missing rocks jutting out from the cliff face. Following her every move, Pips flew beside her. In a final burst of speed, they shot right over the top of the falls. Pips slowed down, but Crysta didn't stop.

She kept on flying. Higher. And higher.

The Beetle Boys roared to a stop some distance away. With their mouths wide open, they watched Crysta head for the canopy.

'Crysta, stop!' yelled Pips.

'She wouldn't do it, would she?' shouted Stump.

Then, to their horror, Crysta disappeared. She completely disobeyed fairylore and flew straight through the canopy.

*But the butterfly
still didn't reply. It
wasn't worried
about a thing.*

4

ABOVE THE CANOPY

Crysta was blinded by the intense light above the canopy. But when her eyes adjusted to the glare, she stared in amazement at the scene in front of her. She'd never seen so much sky. It was so blue, and it went on for ever and ever.

White puffy clouds drifted above her; below, the treetops stretched to the horizon like a soft, green, mossy carpet. Never in her wildest dreams had she pictured the world above the canopy to be so beautiful, or so quiet.

She soaked up the warmth of the sun, breathed in the clear fresh air and stretched her wings. She flew across the treetops, twisting and twirling, enjoying a freedom she'd only ever dreamt about. Then, daring to explore further, she soared upwards, spiralling, tumbling, free-falling, riding the breeze.

From high in the sky, she noticed a towering rock

far off in the distance. A thin, black swirling cloud rose from one side of it. Crysta had never seen a rock that was taller than a tree, or a cloud that rose from the ground.

'What a strange mist,' she thought to herself. But before she had more time to think about it, the sky around her darkened.

Looking up, she froze in horror. A huge peregrine falcon was plummeting out of the clear blue sky, its gleaming, deadly talons stretched out towards her. She screamed as the falcon reached to grab her, and dived for the canopy.

Her heart beating faster than her wings, she flew like the wind, disappearing back down through the trees. But the falcon didn't want to lose her. It followed her, with a crash of broken branches, into the forest; it was so close behind her she could feel its breath on her wings.

'May the angels of Sol protect me!' she cried, dodging a shower of broken branches and falling leaves. Desperately looking around her, she saw a chance for escape—a tiny opening in a maze of prickly vines hanging down in front of her. With her wings tucked close by her side, she covered her face with her hands and dived through the opening.

When she shot out the other side, she knew she was safe. The falcon dived after her, but the dense vines tore its wings. Squealing angrily, it flapped around until it was free, then headed back to the open sky.

Crysta didn't look back, nor did she slow down. Her heart pounding, she sped through the forest. In her blind dash from the falcon, she didn't see Pips until she crashed into him, bowling them both head over heels in a flurry of twisted wings.

'Ooohhh!' they yelled, tumbling through the air.

'What are you trying to do? Kill me?' Pips bellowed, finding Crysta wrapped up in his arms.

'That was too close for comfort,' she cried, clinging to him.

'You could have got us all killed!' shouted Stump, noisily revving his beetle.

'Yeah! We were almost falcon fodder,' yelled Knot.

'So, what did you see up there, Crys?' asked Pips.

But Crysta didn't reply. She flew out of his arms and disappeared through the trees, towards the Antarctic beech forest. She just had to tell Magi Lune what she'd seen.

She found Magi floating in her aerial garden, tending to her rare seedlings. But when Crysta tried to describe what she'd seen above the canopy, she had trouble finding the right words.

Magi Lune sighed. 'The rock you saw was Mount Warning, and the mist you describe was probably smoke.'

Crysta had never heard of smoke, and Magi's explanation, that smoke is the cloud of fire, only added to her confusion. 'But what's fire?' she wanted to know.

Magi told her that fire was something that didn't happen in the rainforest because it was too wet.

'But isn't the whole world wet?' Crysta asked.

'There are many things in our world you don't yet know about, Crysta. But you don't have to fly above the canopy to learn about them,' Magi replied, fumbling through the pockets of her robe. Then, holding out a tiny seed, she explained that some of those things were far away, some were deep inside her heart... and others were right under her nose.

To Crysta's amazement, the seed floated out of Magi's hand towards her. Goggle-eyed, she watched it hang in mid-air.

'That's incredible!'

'There are worlds within worlds, Crysta,' Magi said, as a leaf and several tiny pebbles also defied gravity and floated into the air, joining the seed. As Crysta watched, a miniature replica of the solar system revolved before her eyes.

'Whatever you saw above the canopy, no matter how strange it seemed, is a part of our world,' said Magi.

Crysta watched spellbound as the seed grew larger and changed colour, until it was blue like the sky and dotted with wispy white clouds. Magi Lune's words were crystal-clear, but they sounded far away. Crysta knew Magi was leading her into a magical dimension—through a tiny seed she was being shown a larger world, one that was dotted with mountains and rivers and vibrant green forests.

'It's so beautiful!'

'Remember, Crysta, everything in creation is connected,' continued Magi. 'That is the magic of life. From the solar system to our own planet, right down to this forest and into a tiny seed, everything in creation is connected to everything else. Never forget, we are all a part of the magic web of life.'

Magi stopped talking, and the dream-like vision ended.

Dazed by what she'd just experienced, Crysta reached out and plucked the seed out of the air. The pebbles and the leaf immediately fell back to the ground.

Magi chuckled at Crysta's look of disappointment,

then told her that the web of life was held together by a delicate balance of forces. Taking the seed from her, Magi placed it on top of a jagged, dead tree stump, where it instantly started to grow.

Crysta was thrilled to see the plant growing so magically, but when Magi asked her to help, the plant shrivelled up the moment she touched it. Crysta was heartbroken, and desperately wanted to know what she'd done wrong.

'You were trying *too* hard,' Magi said, reviving the plant. 'Everyone can call on the power of nature. It's within us all. But you'll have to discover your own way to use it. Remember, it's a gentle power.'

Magi handed Crysta another seed. She told her to plant it somewhere safe in the forest and to look after it. Crysta tucked this seed carefully inside her cobweb pouch and agreed to come back and tell Magi how the seed was growing.

But once Crysta left, Magi Lune allowed worry to cloud her face. Birds flew down to comfort her, and a branch of the newly grown fig tree reached down and lifted her high into the forest. One by one the trees parted, until there was a long leafy tunnel stretching through them.

At the end of this tunnel, Mount Warning was visible. A thick column of dark smoke rose from the base of the dark mountain.

With a terrible sense of foreboding, Magi knew only too well what that dark smoke meant.

5

CRYSTA IN TROUBLE

Crysta flew slowly home via Sleepy Hollow. She stopped to rest beside the rock she called Stoneface. She needed time to think about what Magi Lune had told her, and this was the place in the forest she always came to when she needed to be by herself. She found comfort in the ancient moss-covered rock with its wise old face etched in stone.

'It's not easy being different, is it?' she asked her silent friend. 'Do you think I'm wrong to be so curious, or should I be content with the way things are, like you?'

Then, remembering the tiny seed Magi Lune had given her, she dug into her pouch and held it up.

'See, I brought you something special, like I said I would! It's a hoop pine, or at least it will be when it grows,' she said, digging a hole in the soil beside Stoneface.

'Let's call it Little Hoop, and we'll look after it

together,' she said. 'I can't help things grow as fast as Magi Lune, but she says that if I practise, I'll be able to do all the things she can do. Maybe I'll even be able to hear you talk! But for now, I want Little Hoop to grow into the tallest tree in Sleepy Hollow.'

After she'd planted the seed, she waved goodbye to Stoneface and continued her flight home.

The sun was well overhead when she arrived back at the towering strangler fig tree known as *Old Hi Rise*. She noticed there was more activity around it than usual. Young fairies were playing a game of 'slide' down the smooth, buttressed roots of the tree, while others sat on low branches, singing as they wove fallen blossoms into a flower chain. Young elves played tag with butterflies, while older elves pruned dead leaves from plants and trees.

Two baby possums, Poss and Gloss, were snuggled up in the fork of the tree beside a young sugar-glider the elves called Slider. Crysta dug into her pouch and produced a tiny spray of succulent new leaves she'd brought back for the baby possums.

Greeney, a long tree snake, was waiting for her.

'Crysssta, you've causssed quite a ssstorm thisss morning,' he said.

'Crysta, everyone's saying you're going to be grounded,' said Slider, gliding towards her. 'But don't worry, if you are grounded, you can always fly with me.'

'Oh Slider, is it as bad as that?'

'Honeyberry, you are in one big heap of trouble,' Blackbeak, a black palm cockatoo, squawked from above. 'The whole of FernGully is talking about your antics this morning. But I must say, I'm proud of you, it's about time someone had a bit of fun in this forest.'

'Thanks, Blackbeak,' she said, fanning herself with her wings as she sat down beside him.

Granny Belladonna leant out of her tiny vine-covered window. 'Crysta, was that you I saw this morning with the Beetle Boys? I don't know what's happening in the forest these days,' she said, shaking her faded old wings. 'No respect for the old ways!'

Ignoring Granny's familiar scolding, Crysta asked Blackbeak if he'd seen Pips.

'He's been and gone,' replied Blackbeak, peering at her with his one good eye. 'He said the Elders are furious. They're all waiting for you inside.' He nodded his hooked beak towards Crysta's front door. 'Pips told me about your trip through the canopy. Sugar-face, you mustn't fly up there. It's too dangerous.'

'If the Elders are waiting for me, I must be in big trouble. What am I going to do?'

'Hang with me and have a nut,' Blackbeak suggested.

'Stop dropping food into my nest,' squawked a green catbird from her staghorn nest below them.

'Oh, go suck eggs!' said Blackbeak rudely.

'Don't you two ever stop arguing?'

'Queenie would be a lonely old bird without me around,' Blackbeak cackled. 'By the way, Pips said he wouldn't tell anyone else about your canopy caper.'

'Thank goodness for that!' Crysta sighed, rearranging her faded snakeskin leotard. She wished Greeney would shed another skin soon. She knew she needed another outfit, but she hated wearing flower petals like the other fairies, because they slowed her down too much. Twisting her hair into a knot on top of her head, she held it in place with a dainty violet she'd picked up in the forest. She only hoped it made her look more fairy-like.

She slowly opened the glowing fungus door in the trunk of *Old Hi Rise.* She took a deep breath when she heard raised voices echoing up the long spiral staircase. Her father, her grandfather and two old elves called Jips and Elwood were in the middle of a heated argument.

At the bottom of the stairs, she peeped through a carved doorway and saw that her living room was crowded with fairies and elves.

In one corner of the room sat her two sisters, Lily and Fern, and her mother. The dance teacher, Rose Myrtle, was comforting Fern, who was crying.

'What you abuse, you lose!' said Elwood sternly.

'Leave this to me, I'll talk to her. It won't happen again,' replied Grandfather Ash, pacing worriedly back and forth, his drooped wings poking through his leaf waistcoat.

'She's had more than enough chances already! I say she loses her wings,' continued Elwood.

Crysta chose this moment to step into the room. Everyone fell silent, and turned to face her.

'Crysta, you've caused a lot of trouble this morning,' said her father, coming towards her. 'Everyone's complained. You were up again at the crack of dawn. Rose Myrtle says you missed another dance class. You were seen speed-flying with a lorikeet, and what were you doing skylarking with those dreadful Beetle Boys?'

'We were only having fun,' she said quietly.

'We don't know what to do with you, Crysta,' said Jips, the most senior of the Elfin Elders. 'You should be grounded. But no-one wants to see that happen. However, we must have your promise that you'll

respect fairylore and leave skylarking to the birds.' His
kind eyes met Crysta's. 'No-one doubts your love for
this forest, but you are too headstrong, and your
curiosity will get you into trouble. It's time you
became more responsible.'

'Magi Lune says...' she began. But Elwood quickly
interrupted her.

'Magi Lune is old! Her ways are ancient. Better you
spend more time helping in the forest than
daydreaming about long-forgotten magic.' He tugged
his long white beard. His pointed ears quivered
nervously as he continued. 'While you were out
skylarking, a falcon flew into the forest. Now there is a
gaping hole in the canopy, and we all know how
dangerous that is.'

Crysta felt miserable, for she knew only too well
that it had all been her fault.

'Well, what do you have to say for yourself, Crysta?'
her father asked.

'I think...' she began nervously, 'I think, there is
something much more dangerous in the forest at the
moment than a hole in the canopy.'

The room became deadly quiet.

'And just what do you mean by that?' demanded
Elwood at last.

Crysta took a deep breath before answering. 'I think
Hexxus is back, and working the weather.'

'Hexxus!' gasped the Elders.

'Crysta, your imagination is out of control!' said her
father sternly. 'Hexxus was from another time and
age. A legend best forgotten. If this is your idea of a
joke...'

'Papa, I've seen things,' she insisted, 'even the frogs
think...'

'Frog talk!' bellowed Elwood. 'Surely you don't believe frog talk!'

Now everyone began to talk at once.

Jips took her aside, and asked her quietly, 'What is it that you've seen, Crysta?'

But before she could answer, Lily joined them.

'Crysta, why do you have to upset everyone all the time? Mother's worried sick that you're going to hurt yourself.'

'Lily,' whispered Crysta, steering her sister to a hollow underneath the staircase. 'Do you believe in evil spirits?'

Lily was shocked by the question. 'Whatever are you talking about?'

'Spirits that can work the weather, and make smoke and fire.'

Lily frowned. 'You're not making sense. What's happening with you?'

'I don't know,' Crysta said. 'But I do know there's some sort of trouble brewing in this forest, and I'm going to find out what it is.'

6
BATTY KODA

The meeting with the Elders ended when Crysta promised to act more responsibly, and she flew off to find Pips.

As she cruised through the forest, she breathed a sigh of relief that she hadn't been grounded. The thought of living in the forest without having the freedom to fly through it was too awful to even think about! She fluttered gracefully around the trees, enjoying the tangy scent of damp leaves and sweet wild ginger.

She dropped in at Sleepy Hollow and was surprised to see that the tiny seed she'd planted had already sprouted into a healthy seedling. She hovered over the little plant, gently touching it. 'Hope I don't shrivel it up,' she said, grinning at Stoneface. But to her surprise, it immediately doubled its size! She couldn't believe it.

'Don't let anyone come near it,' she said to the rock. 'There's magic happening here. I'm going to grow the tallest tree in the whole forest, you just wait and see.'

Of course Stoneface didn't reply, but Crysta just knew he was as excited as she was. She leapt into the air, somersaulted backwards and looped the loop. Then she waved goodbye to Little Hoop and Stoneface, promising to come back as soon as she could, and set off again to find Pips.

She guessed he'd be playing music with his friends Sandy and Wilkea down by Mossy Bank, and she was right. But they weren't playing alone. Hundreds of birds had gathered around them and they were all singing and flapping along to the music.

Sandy was belting out a loud rhythm on a set of fungi drums, while young Wilkea played the flute. She noticed Wilkea had become a lot more confident since he'd started playing music with Pips and Sandy. Wilkea had been born without wings, but now that he was playing music all the time, he didn't seem to worry about his handicap.

Pips was strumming a long, stringed instrument that looked like a dried pea-pod. A crowd of frogs of all shapes and sizes was croaking to the beat, and Al, a lyrebird, was mimicking all the sounds. The noise was so deafening that Crysta had to cover her ears.

When Pips saw her fluttering overhead, he flew towards her. Still playing his pea-pod, he shouted over the music without missing a note.

'That was a crazy thing you did this morning. To fly above the canopy and then to buzz off without saying why, was a very sluggy thing to do. You need your wings clipped.'

'I didn't come here to argue with you,' she shouted back. 'I came to ask for your help. But I can see that's a waste of time.'

And with these words, she turned and flew away.

'Hey, slow down!' yelled Pips, slipping his pea-pod over his shoulder and flying after her. 'I want to know what the Elders had to say.'

'They said I should get serious!'

He laughed. 'About time!' he said, chasing her through the trees.

'. . . And stop hanging out with bug-brained layabouts like you.'

Laughing, she stopped to rest on a fungus platform attached to the side of a tall booyong tree. 'Thanks for not telling them about my trip through the canopy,' she said to him. Then, looking up and down the tree to make sure she wasn't overheard, she told Pips that she was planning to fly to Mount Warning and asked him to join her.

Pips couldn't believe he'd heard her properly. 'Crysta, Mount Warning doesn't exist. It's only a place in fairy legend.'

'No, it's not, Pips! Mount Warning is at the edge of this forest.'

'But there is no edge to this forest,' he replied, deeply shocked by what she'd said.

'I know that's what we've been told,' she whispered. 'But it isn't true. Pips, I've seen Mount Warning and it isn't very far away at all! Please say you'll come with me!'

But before Pips could answer, a piercing scream of sheer terror filled the forest and before they knew what had happened, a huge flying creature crashed into their tree, ripping their little fungus platform out from under them.

Crysta yelled as she was flung out of the tree, but Pips grabbed her in mid-air and pulled her along after him.

'We've got to follow it!' he shouted.

'What is *it*?' she asked, wide-eyed.

'Don't know, but let's find out.'

Speeding through the trees, they followed a trail of broken branches.

'Whatever it is, it's heading straight towards *Old Hi Rise*,' Crysta shouted.

'I think it's some sort of bat!' said Pips.

'It's going to kill itself!'

'And everyone else in the forest, unless we stop it,' he replied.

Pips dashed ahead of her, but before he could reach it, the frantic bat bounced off one tree, hit another, then disappeared inside the hollow trunk of *Old Hi Rise*. Fairies and elves began diving out of doorways and hollows.

'We've been hit!' squawked Blackbeak. 'Everyone evacuate, fly for your lives!'

'Pips, we've got to save that bat,' Crysta called, dodging fleeing fairies and flying into the hollow at the base of the tree. But she was totally unprepared for what was inside. It was pitch dark, and she was in real danger of being squashed by the terrified bat.

In desperation, she closed her eyes and chanted loudly:

Bless your heart with magic light,
I give the gift of fairy sight.

A sudden blast of glowing light filled the dark hollow. To Crysta's amazement, the bat immediately calmed down and turned towards her. He smiled a lopsided smile. 'You're a strange little bug,' he said, before he fainted.

'It worked!' cried Crysta, bending over him and fanning him with her wings. 'I did it! I worked a magic spell!'

Everyone gathered around to see for themselves what had just crashed into their lives.

'That's no ordinary bat,' Pips whispered, poking his head into the hollow tree trunk. 'What's happened to this poor creature? Where on earth has he come from?'

No-one could answer this question. It was certainly the strangest bat any of them had ever seen. Between them, the elves dragged him out into the open air. It was obvious that he was in a bad way. He was scratched and bleeding and covered in prickly ash. But the strangest thing about him were the two antennae, one sticking out of either side of his bald head.

As everyone peered at him, the bat opened his eyes and shrieked. Crysta did her best to reassure him that he was safe, but he wouldn't stop shivering. His antennae clicked together and sparked alarmingly, and he started to speak in such a garbled way that no-one understood a word he said. Things like, 'Gimme gamma inspiration' and 'Pass the probe' made absolutely no sense to anyone.

'Well, isn't this a bit of the unusual?' Crysta's father muttered nervously.

'Father, I gave him fairy sight with my magic. It worked, I fixed him.'

'Did you now,' he replied, staring at the bat's spinning eyeballs. 'Well, don't fix anybody else!'

The bat continued to chatter incoherently. The

crowd of fairies and elves moved closer.

'It's all right, they won't hurt you,' said Crysta, gently stroking him. Responding to her touch, the bat finally relaxed a little.

'Do you have a name, friend?' asked Grandfather Ash. The bat looked to Crysta for reassurance, and she smiled at him.

'It's all right,' she said. 'I promise no-one's going to hurt you.'

The antennae clicked together. 'The name is Koda, Batty Koda. I'm a cosmic quavo. A nocturnal, placental, flying mammal. A part of the family Did-i, or Didn't-i. A bat in fact, is where I'm at.'

'And where did you say you were from, Batty?' Grandfather Ash asked. But once again, Batty exploded into gibberish.

'From? . . . where is anybody from?' he jabbered. 'The chicken or the egg? But that's a scrambled idea!' Flapping his wings, he started hopping from one leg to the other in a crazy dance. The fairies and elves backed away and watched his performance in stunned silence. He began to wail.

'I'm a freak from a labora-tree
A freaky fruit bat as you can see.
But now I'm here and flappin' free
And my story will tell you what happened to me!
I've been brain-fried, electro-wired,
Infected and injected and terrified.
I've been flatlined and disconnected,
Mummified and resurrected.
Sure, I'm a dingbat, but I'm a cool cat
'Cause I'm a fruit bat, that's where I'm at.
Now, hang a fang while I flap my jaw,
Excuse the slang and I'll tell you more.

I'm rude, I'm nude, I'm even tattooed,
I'm scatty Batty Koda, one groovy dude.
I've been bent out of whack and immunised,
Polarised and sterilised...
Hypnotised and humanised...'

'*Humans?*' Crysta cried. 'Did you say *humans?*'

Now the crowd of fairies and elves all started talking at the tops of their voices. It seemed everyone remembered something about humans from the old human-tales. That is, all except Paddy, who was a baby pademelon and still lived inside his mother's pouch and didn't know much about anything.

'What's a human-tale?' he asked.

'Don't know,' his mother replied nervously. 'But I'm sure it wouldn't be as long as ours.'

'I know what humans were like,' called Granny Belladonna. 'They were friendly spirits who lived in the sky.'

'No. They didn't live in the sky,' replied Rose Myrtle. 'They lived deep in the earth.'

'I always thought they lived in the water,' said Lily.

To quieten everyone down, the three Elfin Elders stepped forward.

'Humans are extinct!' shouted Elwood.

'Long gone,' agreed Jips.

'Vanished,' said Grandfather Ash.

But this information only added to the arguments about humans and where they'd vanished to.

Crysta was the only one who didn't join in. She sat beside Batty Koda and tried to comfort him. She told him she'd look after him, and that FernGully would be his new home. She remembered what Magi Lune had told her about healing, and she soothed his wounds with a mixture of leaves that stopped the stinging and the bleeding.

'You're groovacious,' Batty suddenly blurted out. 'You're the sweetest little bug I've ever seen.'

Crysta giggled. 'I'm not a bug, I'm a fairy! My name's Crysta.'

'Fairy-bug, fairy-bug. Crystabellis, the fairy-bug,' he chanted, grinning.

'Did you *really* see humans? Were they at Mount Warning?' Crysta asked him. But Batty refused to tell her. He started to shiver violently and wouldn't say anything except, 'Short-circuit side-effects! Change the channel! Fractured figs, fairy-bug, forget about humans and forget all about Mount Warning.'

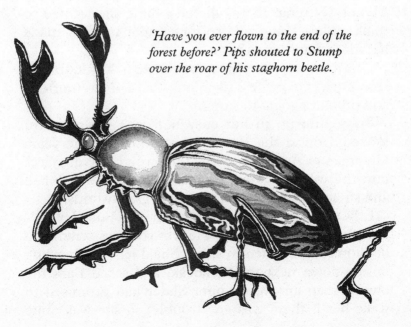

'Have you ever flown to the end of the forest before?' Pips shouted to Stump over the roar of his staghorn beetle.

7

A SECRET JOURNEY

Crysta had no intention of forgetting about Mount Warning. It was the *only* thing she wanted to think about. Being told to forget about it only made her more determined to go.

That night, as she hopped into her cobweb hammock, she made a decision. 'I'm going tomorrow, and no-one's going to stop me!'

Snuggling up in her cosy bed, she yawned and looked around the sleeping hollow. Over the years Grandfather Ash had polished the wood, carving faces into the wooden knots so that at night they winked and smiled by the light of flickering glow-worms.

Lily and Fern were sound asleep, but Crysta's thoughts were with Batty. He was so brain-scrambled he didn't know when to sleep. She'd left him hanging upside-down next to Blackbeak, and asked Bark the owl to keep an eye on him. Slider had promised to wake her if there was any trouble, so she was quite sure Batty was safe for the night.

As she drifted off to sleep, she heard the gentle patter of rain against the leaves.

A collection of hazy images floated before her, of distant mountains swirling in mist, of ancient moss-covered trees, and of dancing bats. Magi's voice drifted in and out of these dreams... 'There are worlds within worlds, Crysta', she heard her say, reminding her of a magic she couldn't quite remember.

She woke to the sound of bird calls. The overnight rain had freshened the forest and the foliage was shimmering with bright raindrops. She dressed quickly, making sure she remembered her cobweb pouch. She hung it from a leaf belt she borrowed from Lily, hoping Lily wouldn't miss it when she woke up.

When she stepped outside her doorway, she found the branch so crowded she could hardly move. Batty was hanging upside down, still wide awake and very much the centre of attention. Two king parrots were feeding him fresh figs, while Blackbeak was trying to persuade him to eat the nuts he was cracking. Slider was chatting to him about hang-gliding, while Greeney was curled around the branch, closely examining Batty's headgear.

'Fairy-bug!' Batty grinned when he saw her. 'I'm on gravity gross-out, this place is incredibulge!'

'And you look like a figged-out disaster! Come on, I think it's time to test your wings. Let's see if you can still fly after all that food.'

'Groovacious!' He grinned. 'Let's hoon!'

Dropping off the branch, he followed her obediently. But he bounced off so many trees and plants that Crysta felt dizzy watching him.

'Rip snort, what a rort! I'm fanging on the wild side,' he yelled, colliding with everything in his path.

'Come on, you're flapping around like a broken branch. We'll never leave *Old Hi Rise* at this rate,' she called out. Then, after several more practice runs, he was up and away.

'Look at me, I'm hooning on the infra-reds! I'm flappin' free,' he bleeped, flying clumsily behind her. 'He-he-hey! Where are we going?'

'Mount Warning,' she called over her shoulder.

Hearing these words, Batty crashed into a giant blackapple tree.

'Fractured figs, fairy-bug. Scared me there. For a moment I thought you said we were going to Mount Warning.'

'I did,' said Crysta, disentangling him from the tree.

'But there are *humans* on Mount Warning,' he whispered.

'Exactly!'

'Sonic interference! Are we on the same wavelength, little sprite? Tread some air, wing away, head for the canopy. *Is this getting through to you?* Mount Warning is the last place in the world a fairy-bug like you wants to go. Why do you think they call it Mount Warning? If it was a nice place they'd call it Mount Let's-have-a-picnic. Look at me—I wasn't born with this stuff sticking out of my head. Nature didn't do this to me. Let's just hang a fang, and talk about this.'

But when Crysta replied, her expression was serious. 'You can stay if you want to. But I'm going.'

'Listen, let's just change this flight plan and flap around here,' Batty pleaded. 'You've got a great set of wings. We could have some fun.'

Crysta didn't answer him, she just kept on flying.

She was determined to reach Mount Warning. She wanted to see the Hexxus tree, she wanted to see smoke; the thought that she might even see a human only added to her determination.

So, when Batty finally realised he wasn't going to change her mind, he flapped along unhappily beside her.

The sun shone directly overhead and the forest was dripping and steaming. After a while Batty relaxed, stopped crashing into so many trees, and started to enjoy himself.

Flying further than she'd ever flown before, Crysta dodged tall black bean and sharp lawyer cane, and helped steer Batty around the twisted branches of giant stinging trees. They listened to parrots squawking, and Batty made Crysta laugh when he tried to mimic a whipbird's short, piercing call.

Every now and again Crysta raced ahead of Batty, chasing flocks of small robins and honey-suckers, her turquoise wings sparkling against the dark forest greens. The time passed quickly, and it was well past noon when Batty insisted they stop for a rest.

'Fairy-bug, it's time to hang a fang. I'm a victim of elemental exhaustion. It's time to suck some juice. I'm zeroed out.'

'All right,' Crysta said. 'But not for too long.'

Fluttering down to the forest floor, she found a dry, leafy place to sit.

'Walk to work . . . walk to work . . . walk to work,' chirped a little voice.

'Listen, Batty. A noisy pitta bird's talking to us.'

'Let's stay here. I like it here,' said Batty, settling against a tree trunk.

'Excuse me,' a gravelly voice sounded from behind

the tree. 'It's not safe to sit on the ground.'

An angle-headed dragon poked his head around the tree and stiffened his pointy spikes.

'Fractured figs, I'm semi-quavered!' shrieked Batty, flapping into the air.

Crysta laughed. 'Draggs! What are you doing here? You've scared my friend.'

'Sorry, Crysta, but you know I can't help the way I look. I seem to scare everyone.'

'Why do you have to look so fierce, when you're really such a softie?'

'Better that way round than the other,' he replied in his gentle voice. 'Now, tell me what you're doing here—you shouldn't be so far from home, Crysta.'

'I'm going to Mount Warning with my friend.'

'Don't know where that is,' he replied, flicking his armour-plated tail. 'But you shouldn't go any further than this, it isn't safe.'

When Crysta asked him what he meant, he couldn't really explain.

'There's something in the air,' he told her. 'Things aren't normal when the earth is heard to grumble. Everyone around here is too nervous to stay. You should go back to FernGully right away.'

Batty agreed, nodding his head furiously. 'Excellent plan, I like that plan, I'm behind that plan one hundred per cent.'

But Crysta wasn't afraid. She assured the angle-headed dragon that they would be home before dark.

'Just make sure you are,' he said, as they flew away.

'This trip is a first-class master disaster,' Batty muttered unhappily.

But Crysta wasn't unhappy, she was bubbling with excitement. She couldn't wait to reach the edge of the forest.

8

THE SILENT FOREST

It took much longer to get to the edge of the forest than Crysta had expected. A violent storm sent them scuttling for shelter. Batty thought they were going to be blown to pieces.

'This is a master blaster,' he bleeped, hanging upside down on a branch, cocooned in his wings.

'It's only a thunderstorm,' Crysta said, shivering and snuggling up against him.

'It's trying to tell us something,' stuttered Batty, peeping out from under his wing. 'It's trying to b-b-blow us b-b-back to where we came from!'

'It's only the wind devils, and they can't hurt us,' Crysta told him, repeating what her grandfather had told her many times before. 'The wise Biami lets the wind devils loose to clean up the forest and freshen the air.'

'Then why do they have to f-f-flatten everything?'

'They're only doing their job,' she said, hoping she sounded more confident than she felt. 'Grandfather says that what's meant to grow, regrows.'

'Fairy-bug, if this Biami is so wise, then why doesn't he stop them going so wild?' asked Batty, wrapping his wings around her to protect her from heavy rain.

'Guess they're not called wind "devils" for nothing,' she whispered. Crysta had never been out in a storm alone, and although she wasn't about to admit it, she was frightened.

Just when they thought the wind was going to blow them out of the tree, there was a blinding flash of lightning, followed by a loud clap of thunder, and the storm suddenly blew over. For the moment all was quiet, and the only sign of the storm was the trail of destruction it had left behind.

'I hate storms,' shivered Batty. 'Let's wing back to FernGully. I don't like it here.'

'I think that's a good idea,' said a soft voice.

'Who said that?' asked Crysta, looking around.

'Me. And I'm right here under your nose,' chuckled the whispery voice.

'Then come out, whoever you are!'

'You don't like it when you can't see things your own way, do you?' teased the voice. 'Remember, there's more to life than meets the eye.'

'All I can see is a soggy old tree,' grunted Batty, drying his wings. 'Let's hoon, this place gives me the creeps.'

'You were pleased enough to find us when the storm hit,' the voice said.

'Oh, Batty, I think it's the tree who's talking to us!'

'Well, I'll be infra-red! Didn't think they *could*.'

'Everything living has something to say, and I can

44

assure you, we're all alive and well in this grove,' another tree rustled gently.

'We certainly are,' whispered another.

'We're the Talking Trees,' explained yet another, 'and we aren't called that for nothing.'

'I've never seen trees like you before,' said Crysta.

'That's because you live in the heart of the Great Forest, and we live on the edge,' they rustled.

'Is *this* the edge of the forest?' asked Crysta excitedly.

'Almost,' the first tree swayed.

'Not quite,' whispered another.

'Let's say it's the end of the Great Forest,' replied the first. 'You see, beyond the Plain of Xanthorrhoeas, where the mountain stands tall, the forest starts again.'

'That's where we're going. To Mount Warning.'

'No, no, no, no, no!' bleeped Batty. 'This is the end of the web, fairy-bug.'

'Be careful,' whispered the first tree. 'The open plain is dangerous for one so small, and there are strange stories about the forest on the other side.'

'I'll be careful. Come on, Batty, we're almost there.'

'It's a waste of time, fairy-bug,' he replied, stubbornly refusing to leave the tree. 'I like it here. We should stay here.'

''Bye,' she called, flying away.

'Hey, come back!' he yelled, dropping off the branch and flapping after her. 'Fractured figs, fairy-bug. I vitally recommend a reassessment of your intentions,' he bleeped, following her trail through the trees. 'I know heaps about humans. I could tell you more than you'd ever want to know. Have I shown you my tattoos?'

But Crysta was far too excited to slow down. Now, for the first time, there was no canopy overhead. The trees thinned rapidly as the land dropped away. Suddenly Crysta and Batty burst into the dazzling sunlight.

'Wow!' cried Crysta, looking at the vast open Plain of Xanthorrhoeas stretching out before her. Beyond the plain towered the dark shape of Mount Warning.

'Sonic interference!' shrieked Batty, streaking back to the nearest tree.

'Batty, come back. There's nothing to be afraid of. It isn't dangerous. It's just different.'

But Batty was hanging upside down, well wrapped up in his wings.

'What's wrong?' she asked, peeping inside them.

'I'm on gravity gross-out. Do you think we could stop and rest for oh, say, about ten years?' he begged. 'Why don't you stay here with me?'

'It's okay, really. I'll be right back,' she said, disappearing into the bright sunlight.

In front of her stretched the Plain of Xanthorrhoeas. 'If I can just get across the plain, I'll be all right,' she said to herself as she tried to judge the distance to the other side. But the whole world seemed to be spinning at a tremendous speed. Enormous clouds rolled across the sky at such a pace she felt she was flying backwards.

She'd seen xanthorrhoeas before, scattered through the rainforest, but she'd never seen so many in one place. Some were short and stumpy, others were tall and straight, but all of them had a skirt of feathery grass around their rough black trunks. Out of the top of these trunks grew a single magnificent spear. She knew the xanthorrhoeas were ancient and that they took hundreds and hundreds of years to grow just a little bit—but still they never grew as tall as the trees in the forest. They were sometimes called grass trees, and as she heard their rustling skirts in the breeze she wondered if they were talking to each other.

Above her, billowing clouds rolled across the sky. Outside the protection of the forest, she knew she was taking a tremendous risk. With a shiver, she remembered how quickly that falcon had dropped out of a clear blue sky.

When she flew over the pointed spears of the ancient xanthorrhoeas, she could hear they were chanting a song. It was an old song, older than they were. Once she'd heard Magi Lune chant such a sound and it had sounded like a warning. The further she flew across the plain, the louder the song became. Then, unexpectedly, a flock of birds in a terrible panic rushed towards her, sending her spinning.

'Turn around!' squawked a sulphur-crested cockatoo.

'Fly for your life!' screeched another.

'What's happening?' she asked, but the frantic birds didn't stop to reply. She couldn't turn back; she'd already come too far, so she kept on flying.

When she finally reached the forest at the foot of Mount Warning, she was exhausted. Her wings were beating so fast that at first she didn't notice the deadly silence. Mount Warning towered above her, a dark swirling mist covering its peak.

She landed on the branch of a sturdy boxwood tree and she was surprised to find no-one in it. Looking around for some sign of life, she noticed that all the trees were marked with identical red 'X' symbols. Placing her hand on the middle of one red mark, she was puzzled by the lack of feeling in the tree. She'd never felt a living tree so cold. When she pulled back her hand, she was shocked to see it was dripping with a sticky, blood-like resin.

Cautiously, she fluttered from tree to tree, peeping around each one, looking for signs of life. She followed a muddy creek that twisted and turned through overhanging tunnels of lifeless trees. Rounding a bend, she came across the first ugly tree she'd ever seen. It was huge. It stood in a clearing all by itself. It was black, gnarled and bent with age. Absolutely nothing grew around it.

A cold wave of fear chilled her heart and she knew at once she was staring at the Hexxus tree. But when she tried to fly away, she found she couldn't move. Like the trees in the forest, she felt icy cold. She felt as though her life was being sapped out of her.

9

THE GIANT ELF

Time seemed to stand still, and no matter how hard she tried, Crysta could not fly away from the Hexxus tree or break the spell that held her to it.

Then she heard the voice. It came from somewhere deep inside the tree and although it was muffled, she heard it quite plainly. The sound of it made her wings curl.

'When the forest falls,' it growled, 'then I'll be free, to seek the revenge that's due to me.'

The earth grumbled, and the tree shuddered violently. Then, just as suddenly, the forest became deadly quiet again. Crysta fluttered her wings and shot forward, suddenly free of the spell. Her heart thumping, she looked around, but not a leaf stirred. There wasn't even a ripple on the surface of the creek. It had all happened so quickly that she wondered if she'd imagined the whole thing.

She was about to fly back the way she'd come, when the biggest elf she'd ever seen walked out of the forest towards her. He was a giant of a figure, and very heavy-footed. He was dressed differently to anyone Crysta had ever seen—his clothes didn't look like they'd been made from flowers or leaves or spider webbing. His huge feet were covered, and she couldn't imagine what they looked like. His arms and hands were bare, and his fair hair stuck out from under his shiny nut-like hat.

Music seemed to be coming out of his ears, and he was humming to himself. On a wide belt around his waist was what looked like a yellow pouch. Crysta noticed that, like Wilkea, this giant elf didn't have wings. But, apart from his size, she didn't think he looked dangerous. In fact, she thought he looked very happy. She called 'Hello', but he didn't hear her, and when he walked straight past her she knew he couldn't see her, either.

The giant elf walked up to the Hexxus tree. He stopped and examined the loose black bark. Crysta saw a frightened little bug scurry across the bark, and watched the elf raise his hand and squirt the bug with a bright red liquid. The bug turned red as it rushed for safety. Then something very unusual happened— where the red liquid touched the tree, it started to hiss and bubble and boil.

The giant elf gasped and stepped back onto a mossy rock, overbalanced, and landed in the creek. Crysta couldn't help laughing at him, as he floundered about in the water like a long-nosed wombat, until she realised he was trying to save his yellow pouch, which had come off his belt and was floating away.

Unable to help him, she circled his head and

discovered that when she flew in front of his face he noticed her. He squinted, and reached out to grab her. He was so off the mark she could only laugh. She laughed at the way his eyes crossed when he tried to grab her. She wasn't the least bit afraid of him, for she knew she could outdistance him in the twinkling of an eye.

Engrossed by this game, she didn't pay attention to the approaching grumble until it became a loud roar. Riveted to the spot, she looked over her shoulder and glimpsed what looked like an enormous monster charging at the trees.

'Oh!' she screamed, as everything went black.

She felt herself suffocating, and knew that she'd been caught in the giant elf's hands. Then the darkness disappeared when the giant elf opened his hands, and she saw the Hexxus tree swaying behind them.

'Look out!' she screamed, as the gnarled tree toppled towards them. But the elf couldn't see what was happening and he couldn't hear her.

There was only one thing she could do. Closing her eyes, she held out her arms and chanted frantically:

Bless your heart with magic light
I give the gift of fairy size...
No! Fairy sight...fairy sight!

A burst of glowing energy shot out of her hands and she felt herself falling through the air in a flurry of leaves. The falling tree crashed around her. When she opened her eyes, she was amazed to see the unconscious elf stretched out beside her. Only now he was her size!

'Oh, no! I've shrunk him!' she gasped.

The tree continued to shake as another tremendous

roar filled the air. Caught up in the branches, they were being dragged towards the roaring monster. Overwhelmed by a sense of powerlessness, she tried desperately to revive the elf. But the elf could not be moved.

The roar was so deafening that Crysta knew that whatever it was, it was about to eat them. Then a dark shadow engulfed them and lifted them up.

'Oooohhh!' Crysta screamed.

'Don't go, I said. Bad idea, I said. But would you listen? Oh no, oh no, oh no!'

'Batty!' cried Crysta, unable to believe her ears.

'Warped banana corpses, fairy-bug. You must *never* fly out of FernGully again!' Heading back over the Plain of Xanthorrhoeas, Crysta thought Batty's crazy chatter was the most wonderful sound she'd ever heard.

Once they were across the plain, Batty slowed down, and for the first time looked closely at the unconscious elf.

'It's a *human*! It's a *human*!' he shrieked, crashing into a tree, and hurling Crysta and the human into the branches.

'Oh, wow! A human!' Crysta whispered. She inspected the limp, almost lifeless body beside her. He was breathing, but he didn't respond to her touch, not even when she bent over him and brushed his fair hair away from his eyes. She noticed a slender shiny object like a silver leaf sticking out of his belt. She pulled it out and examined it closely.

At this moment the human stirred and opened his eyes. The first thing he saw was his knife pointed dangerously close to his face.

'Take anything you want,' he blurted out. 'I won't

tell the cops.'

'Are you all right?' she asked, waving the knife under his nose.

'I'm fine, I guess,' he nodded, eyeing her nervously. 'Tell me, what's going on here?'

'The monster tried to eat you. But my friend and I saved you.' She smiled, then without another word she disappeared up the tree to look for Batty. She found him lying in a fork of the tree with a stunned expression on his face.

'Sonic interference! What a nightmare. I thought I saw a human.'

Hanging over the branch, he looked below him.

'Aargghh!' he shrieked. 'I did!'

'Is he *really* a human?' Crysta asked, buzzing with excitement.

'Yes!' Batty jabbered. 'Restrain it. Medicate it. Kill it! Kill it!'

A huge goanna was standing in front of him, its long tongue flicking in and out as it eyed him over.

10
ZAK

The human sat up, rubbing his eyes, and looked at the enormous winged creature hanging upside down above him.

'The monster!' he shouted to Crysta. 'Watch out!'

She laughed, flying down to him. 'That isn't a monster, that's my friend, Batty Koda. He's a fruit bat.'

'Could have fooled me,' he replied. 'And what are you supposed to be? Some sort of fairy?'

'Of course I am. What about you? Are you really a human?'

'Last time I checked,' he said, looking around him for the first time. 'Listen, this is too weird, I'm outta here. Time for this dream to end.'

He stood up, turned around and stomped off down the branch and, without thinking, stepped on a leaf which broke off and floated away with him on it.

'Am I dead?' he shouted, as he surfed the leaf through the air.

'No, you're not,' yelled Batty. 'But we can fix that.'

Flying out of the tree, Crysta followed the leaf as it twisted and turned on the breeze.

'Oh, wow!' she squealed. 'This is stupendulous! I can't wait to get you home.'

Riding the breeze like a wave, the human guided the leaf down to the forest floor. But when a giant beetle crawled past him and waved his armour-plated nippers in the air, he screamed at the top of his voice, 'What's happened to me?'

'I shrank you,' said Crysta, watching him land on a pile of sodden leaves. 'I didn't mean to,' she added with a grin, 'it was the most amazing thing. It's not what the spell was supposed to do, but Magi Lune will fix you.'

'You *shrank* me?' He stared at her as he scrambled to his feet.

'Catches on quick, doesn't he?' bleeped Batty.

'Well, *un*shrink me. And I mean now!' he bellowed.

'Well, I guess I could take a bash at it. It might work, but I'm only learning, so you'll have to take your chances.'

'Oh, great! I've been shrunk by an amateur! Okay, bash away.'

Closing her eyes and holding out her arms, Crysta chanted:

What was done, now undo.
Return you to the form that's true.

A blast of energy shot out of her hands. His head blew up to twice its size, then shrank back again. Bits and pieces of him began to grow, but not all at the same time. When the spell stopped, he was still the same size.

'I could try again,' Crysta said, puzzled.

'No way!' he said, shuddering. 'Let's leave this to Magi-whoever-she-is. By the way, I'm Zak,' he said, holding out his hand to her.

Looking at his hand curiously, she replied, 'I'm Crysta.' Then, smiling her most dazzling smile, she added, 'Don't you worry, Zak, I'm going to take you to FernGully. It's the most beautiful place in the forest. You'll love it there. Come on, Batty can carry you.'

'Moi?' bleeped Batty. 'No way! Not this little mammal. Carry a human? I'd rather gargle plutonium.'

'Hey, the feeling's mutual, Batman. I can look after myself,' Zak said, stomping off through the trees. But he didn't get very far before he was bellowing for help.

Crysta found him backed up against the trunk of a giant tallowwood tree. A huge goanna was standing in front of him, its long tongue flicking in and out as it eyed him over.

'Oh, no! Don't eat him,' she cried, flying down between them.

'But I have to eat *some*body,' hissed the goanna, staring Zak straight in the eye.

'Oh, please don't eat my friend,' pleaded Crysta, drooping her wings and fluttering them daintily.

'Oh, little sweet-wings,' said the big goanna, softening at the sight of her. 'You know any friend of a fairy is a friend of mine. Tell you what—if I can't eat him, I can at least give him a lift.' He nodded to Zak. 'Hop on my back.'

Reassured by Crysta that he would be safe, Zak scrambled up on the goanna's back. Then, without a word of warning, the goanna shot off through the forest at top speed, his short but sturdy front and back legs a blur against the undergrowth.

Crysta followed close behind, while Batty flapped unhappily overhead.

'Fractured figs, fairy-bug,' he cursed. 'This is a calamitous collision of uncalculated circumstances—a first-class master disaster!'

The goanna kept to the creek, running under ferns and bracken and scrambling over fallen logs. Every now and again, when he saw something worth eating, he scrambled up tree trunks. Crysta was impressed by the way Zak clung on.

Just before dusk, the goanna stopped and dropped Zak off.

'This is as far as I'm going,' he hissed in his deep voice. 'If you follow the creek you'll find your way to FernGully.'

'Thanks,' said Zak, only too happy to get off and stretch his legs. 'That was the craziest ride I've ever been on.'

He wanted to rest, but Crysta insisted that they keep moving. As she walked beside him she could hardly contain her excitement.

'I've got so many questions to ask you,' she said, copying his long stride. 'Tell me, why have humans returned to the forest? And who was that monster eating the trees?'

Zak laughed at her. 'That wasn't a monster. It was a machine.'

'What's a *masheen*?' she asked, frowning.

'Well, it's a thing for cutting down trees,' he panted, climbing over a fallen log.

'But that's terrible!' she gasped, fluttering ahead of him and pulling him over the log.

'Only if you live in a tree,' he said, grinning. He took her hand.

'But I *do* live in a tree!' she said, quickly pulling her hand away. 'And so do all my friends.'

A massive cluster of bright red toadstools loomed ahead. Zak wound his way around the thick, spongy stalks. The toadstools almost overpowered him with their strong smell. Crysta fluttered overhead and peered down at him from the top of the toadstools.

'Could it come to FernGully?' she asked.

'No way. You've got nothing to worry about,' he said, elbowing his way out of the rubbery tunnel.

'Why?' asked Crysta, flying backwards beside him.

'Because it's . . . it's . . . trapped,' he replied, stumbling over twigs and vines.

'I know!' she cried, lifting up a vine for him to walk under. 'It's trapped by those red marks. It can't go past them. Those red marks must be magic.'

'You're pretty smart, fairy!' He sat down to rest in the darkening forest.

Crysta sat beside him and they watched the night forest flicker to life as, one by one, tiny lights appeared in the trees.

Batty hung upside down from a nearby branch, never taking his eyes off Zak. 'Buzz off! Get off our airwaves, stop scrambling the amplitudes!' he jabbered rudely.

But Zak didn't take any notice of Batty. He couldn't take his eyes off Crysta as she stretched out beside him on the soft carpet of leaves.

'You were protecting the trees,' she said, sighing dreamily. 'No wonder the monster wanted to kill you. I'm so glad humans have returned to the forest to protect the trees.'

'What do you mean, *returned*?' he asked, watching a cluster of glow-worms sparkle in the tree above him.

'You've returned, because you used to live here with us a long time ago. You were our friends. Don't you remember?'

'We did?' He laughed, while Batty shrieked at the top of his voice.

'Friends? Oh, no, fairy-bug. Oh, no, no, no, no, no! Fractured figs, don't zero out now. You've got it all wrong. This thing isn't a friend!'

'Oh, it all makes sense now,' Crysta said, ignoring Batty.

Leaning over Zak, her face close to his, she looked deeply into his eyes and whispered, 'I want to learn magic like yours. Will you teach me?'

11

NIGHT MAGIC

A s night closed in on the forest, Magi Lune began to feel really worried. From the very moment that the Hexxus tree fell, she knew that Hexxus had escaped. She didn't know how, but she could feel his evil presence again. At first it was only a passing feeling, but with the approach of evening, the feeling persisted and grew more intense.

She knew there were humans at the edge of the forest. She'd known that from the moment she'd seen the dark smoke rising from the base of Mount Warning. In the past she'd never had reason to fear them, but these were different humans to the ones she'd known long ago. And, although she couldn't say why, she knew the clouds of smoke meant trouble. An even stronger feeling that these humans had been responsible for the release of Hexxus, added to her concern.

For the first time in her long life, she didn't know exactly what the trouble was, or just what was going on in the forest. But she knew that something was about to happen.

When the sun had set, Magi decided to see if she could find some answers down by the rock pools— tonight there would be a full moon, and she knew that the water in the pools would be crystal-clear and easy to read. As she hurried away from her home Ock and Rock followed close behind her. The giant cassowaries were also worried. They'd never seen her so upset.

But they weren't the only ones who were worried as night fell. Around *Old Hi Rise* there was a great deal of activity, as word got around that Crysta had disappeared. Glow-worm lanterns lit the forest, and fairies and elves gathered around the towering strangler fig tree waiting for news.

'We must organise a search party,' said Jips, taking control of the situation. 'Everyone can join in, especially the night-timers. Everyone who can see well in the dark should start looking now. The rest will have to wait until morning.'

'I'll go and see if there's any sign of her down at the falls,' said Slider, gliding away.

'Does anyone have the faintest idea where she could be?' asked Ash.

'She winged out of here at sunrise with the fruit-grabber,' squawked Blackbeak. 'That's the last I've seen of her.'

'How about you, Pips?' asked Ash. 'You know her better than anyone.'

'Well, she's got her wings in a twist about a lot of things at the moment,' he replied thoughtfully. 'You see, she thinks Hexxus is back, somewhere at the edge of the forest, and she was talking about flying to Mount Warning. But I'm sure she didn't mean it.'

'Mount Warning!' exclaimed Elwood. 'You can't be serious.'

'Why didn't you tell us this earlier?' asked Jips.

'You should have stopped her,' said Elwood, nervously tugging his beard.

'*You* try to stop Crysta doing what she wants to do,' Pips muttered.

'There's no use arguing,' interrupted Grandfather Ash, stepping between Elwood and Pips. 'What's done is done. What's important is *what* we're going to do to find her.'

'What's happening? What's happening?' shouted Granny Belladonna, scrambling down the tree.

'We're organising a search party for Crysta,' Jips told her, steadying her as she landed awkwardly beside him.

'Then I'm coming too,' said Granny. 'I like parties.'

'You can't go, Granny,' said Rose Myrtle. 'It's far too dangerous, and you can't fly very well.'

'Podgobbles to you!' sniffed the old fairy. 'You're not going to leave me out of any party.'

While everyone was discussing what to do, Pips told Sandy he was going to look for Magi Lune. Deciding on a plan of action, he asked Sandy to round up the Beetle Boys. Wilkea said he'd stay and listen to what the Elders had planned. The three young elves agreed to meet at Python Rock when the moon was overhead.

Pips set off without knowing exactly where Magi Lune lived. He rarely went to the Antarctic beech tree forest. A whole mountainside of gloomy old trees wasn't exactly his idea of fun. He'd never understood

Crysta's fascination with this corner of the forest, or with Magi Lune, and he thought any interest in the Old Powers was a complete waste of time.

Now, by the light of the full moon, the moss-covered trees seemed ghostly. Curtains of trailing mist brushed against him, and the hooting of a lonely owl made him feel uneasy.

He was relieved when the trees thinned and he saw a clearing below him. Two huge silhouettes stood beside a circular rock pool. When he flew down to investigate, he saw that they were Ock and Rock. Magi Lune was standing between them. As he neared them, he noticed that the surrounding trees were packed with silent spectators. Owls, possums and sugar gliders were all quietly sitting together. Wondering what he'd flown into, Pips edged onto a crowded branch overhanging the rock pool.

'Did she lose something?' he asked a rare white lemuroid.

'She's looking into the future,' the lemuroid whispered, swinging by her long furry tail. Ock and Rock were also whispering, but their deep voices carried on the still night air.

'There is an unnatural force gathering,' said Rock, as Magi Lune scooped sparkling droplets of water from the pool. 'It's reflected in the waters.'

'What's an unnatural force?' asked Ock.

'Never you mind,' replied Rock importantly. 'You'll know it when you see it.'

'Ask her if she can look a bit harder and tell me where Crysta is,' called Pips. But the big birds told him to be quiet and not disturb Magi.

'There are other things to look for right now,' whispered Rock.

'Like what? Staring into gobs of water?' said Pips impatiently.

'It's not *where* she's looking that's important, it's what she *sees*,' said Ock.

Pips watched Magi Lune move as if in a trance around the pool. She scooped up more silver droplets of water, and these she spun magically in the air.

'Looks like hocus-pocus to me,' said Pips, flying away. 'I've got more important things to do than watch a full moon display of fairy magic. I've got to find Crysta.'

As he flew towards Python Rock, his unease grew. He thought the air felt different and the moon shadows looked eerie.

At the time Pips didn't know it, but in those night shadows lurked Hexxus. Hexxus hadn't been free for very long, but he was growing at a frightening rate. When the tree that had held him prisoner for so long had fallen, he'd suddenly found himself to be a free spirit. At first he was only a wispy, shadowy figure, but he'd unexpectedly found a surprisingly good source of fuel to feed off; one that wasn't available when he'd been on the loose before. It was thick, black oil, and it spilled from the machine the humans were using to cut down the trees.

Hexxus hated humans as much as forests, and fairies, and fresh air and everything else that represented life, but now he discovered there was one thing he liked about humans—their machines!

The oil gave Hexxus substance, and the fumes he inhaled pumped him up, until he was bigger than he'd ever been before. He liked being the size and shape of a dense, black cloud, because it gave him greater scope for destruction.

So, tonight, while the FernGully mob looked for Crysta, Hexxus tested his new-found strength. With his fiery eyes burning, he glided through the forest as a dark swirling mist and killed everything he touched. He discovered that he could kill whole sections of the forest with one blast of his toxic breath. Right now he was really enjoying himself, because he knew it was only a matter of time before he destroyed the whole forest and every living thing in it.

12
WORLDS WITHIN WORLDS

gust of cold, damp wind suddenly reminded Crysta that she needed to find shelter for the night. She'd been so fascinated with Zak she'd forgotten they were still a long way from home, and now they would have to spend the rest of the night in this unfamiliar part of the forest.

Looking for Batty, she saw him hanging upside down, almost hidden, among long strips of bark hanging from a nearby stringy-bark tree.

Leaving him alone, she fluttered off in search of a safe place to sleep. She didn't want to spend the night in a dark and stuffy burrow, she wanted to be high up in the trees where she always felt safe. But Zak's lack of wings posed a problem, and ruled out her usual choices.

She hunted for an empty bird's nest, and checked out empty tree-trunk hollows, but these were either too small or too dark.

A glowing fungus staircase growing up the side of a massive carabeen tree caught her eye. Running up it, she discovered that it ended when it fanned out into a soft platform almost at the top of the tree. With the tree trunk and branches as protection from the wind, she knew they would be safe.

Excited, she hurried back to tell Zak. But when she flew into the clearing, she found the air was thick and heavy with a choking mist. It smelt overpoweringly strong.

Zak was standing in front of a brush turkey mound, which was glowing brightly in the dark.

'Come and warm yourself,' he called. 'I had one of the wonders of modern technology in my pocket—a disposable lighter!' He grinned, holding it up for her to see.

'What is it?' Crysta asked, creeping slowly towards the flame.

'A fire,' he said, proud of his effort.

'That's fire?' She reached out to touch the flame.

'No!' he shouted, pulling her hand back. But she'd already touched the flame, and her hand throbbed with a dull red glow.

'Ow!' she cried, a single tear rolling down her cheek. Zak wiped the tear from her face, and was surprised when it rolled down his finger and lay in the palm of his hand, where it sparkled for a moment before disappearing in a tiny burst of light.

'Oh, no!' shouted Crysta, snapping out of her trance. 'The fire! It's too hot for the brush turkey's eggs.'

'What brush turkey?' asked Zak. But before Crysta had a chance to reply, he was bowled head over heels by a powerful bird, which leapt on top of the mound and with a kick of one of its long legs scattered the glowing embers in all directions.

'There are eggs in that mound,' Crysta cried, pulling Zak out from under a pile of leaves. 'Quickly, follow me, we've got to get off the ground fast, the brush turkey's going wild!'

'Hang a fang, what's a bat got to do to get some sleep around here?' shouted Batty, woken by the uproar.

'It's all right, Batty. Go back to sleep, we'll see you in the morning,' shouted Crysta as she helped Zak up the first step of the fungus staircase. After the first stair it was easy climbing, as the fungus conveniently spiralled up the giant trunk.

'This is incredible!' Zak yelled, running up the stairs behind Crysta. The fungus glowed with an iridescent light, and each stair was individually illuminated. 'I've never seen anything like this before. This is one monster of a tree—what is it?'

'It's a yellow carabeen, but it isn't a monster,' said Crysta. 'This is one of the birds' favourite trees. The bowerbirds, pigeons, doves, catbirds, and most of the parrots in the forest live off the fruit of this tree.'

Gently touching its orangey-brown bark, she smiled.

'All the trees in this forest are my friends. What are the trees like where you live?'

'Not like this,' he replied. 'I live in a city.'

'What's a *siddy*?' she asked, leading the way higher up the tree.

'Oh, you know—buildings, traffic, roads, lights. Not many trees. A city,' he said, stopping to look out over the night-time forest.

'How can you live without trees?' Crysta asked,

climbing up to the soft fungus platform and sitting down.

'Never thought much about it,' he said, climbing up and sitting beside her.

'But the trees give life! They help make the air and the rain,' she said, folding her wings behind her.

'Oh, we've got all *that* stuff.'

'But don't you miss talking with the forest?' she asked, lying back on her arms.

'Can't say I've actually talked to a forest before,' he replied, stretching out beside her. Looking at her in the moonlight, he thought how extraordinary she was. Her dainty, pointed ears and windswept hair framed a face that was both mischievous and totally innocent. And when she was still, her body seemed to be almost transparent.

'I talk to the forest all the time,' she whispered, catching a moonbeam in the palm of her hand and lightly rolling it into a glittering ball.

'What does it say?' Zak asked, watching her weave her fairy magic right under his nose.

'Well, listen then!' she said, blowing the moonbeam off the tip of her finger and closing her eyes.

As the full moon peeped at them through the treetops, and glow-worms twinkled in the leafy shadows, Zak listened to the night. He was surprised to hear the forest hum to a very definite rhythm. Night crickets led a steady chorus, while trees rustled as the wind strummed their leaves. Frogs croaked in time to the crickets and an owl hooted softly in the distance.

'All right! Get down, funky forest! I've never thought of the forest talking or singing before. It's a whole other world up here, isn't it?' he said.

'Magi Lune says there are lots of different worlds,' replied Crysta softly. 'She says some of them we don't ever get to see, but that doesn't mean they don't exist.'

'You're really keen on this Magi character, aren't you?' Zak smiled, rolling onto his side to get a better look at her. 'Is she a fairy, too?'

'Of course she is! What did you think?'

'Well, she could be a witch, I suppose.' They both laughed. 'Didn't you say she had a spell that would fix me?'

'Do you believe in witches?' Crysta asked excitedly.

'No way!' he said, resting his head on his arm. 'I was only kidding. Tell me, what do fairies do all day, when they aren't talking to humans or catching moonbeams?'

She frowned. '*Do*? I don't know what you mean.'

'Well, do you work? Do you have a job?'

'What's a *jawb*?' she asked, stretching her wings and fluttering them daintily.

'How do you spend each day?' he said, looking at her wings and wondering what it would be like to fly.

'Have fun, mostly,' she said with a laugh.

'Yeah? That sounds cool.'

'No, it's usually hot,' she said, tucking her wings behind her.

'No, you've got it wrong. Cool means hot.'

'Whatever do you mean?'

'You know—cool, bodacious, bad, tubular. You know, like you are one cool babe,' he said, holding her hand.

'Is that good?'

'Totally.' He grinned. '*Now* we're communicating.'

'That's tubular,' she said, bursting into laughter as she said the word.

For a long time they lay side by side in silence, happy and relaxed in each other's company. Lost in their own thoughts, they listened to the forest talk and watched the moon glide slowly through the trees. Finally, exhausted after their long day, they drifted off to sleep.

They slept so soundly that neither of them stirred when a sinister, shadowy hand trailed across the moon, darkening the forest. Neither of them had any idea that everything that this sinister shadow fell upon suddenly shrivelled and died. And they were so sound asleep they didn't hear the earth groan with a deep and heart-wrenching call. The cruel laughter that echoed on the breeze would have chilled their hearts if they'd heard its deadly message.

'Honeyberry, you are
in one big heap of
trouble,' Blackbeak, a
black palm cockatoo,
squawked from above.

13

THE SEARCH PARTY

Pips and Sandy flew through the moonlit forest beside the Beetle Boys. Pips was glad of their company, but he wished they weren't quite so rowdy. Knot had let Wilkea ride on the back of his beetle, so he had been able to join in the search too.

At Eagles' Corner they took the left bank of the gully then flew past a labyrinth of rocky caves high above Stoney Creek. Pips and Sandy knew this area well. They often played here—it was one of the longest and clearest free falls in the forest and perfect for skydiving. It was also where the Beetle Boys lived.

Pips hoped that Stump wasn't going to recruit any more of his gang. But tonight most of their caves were empty, and with the exception of a few lone sleeping beetles, all was quiet.

'Have you ever flown to the end of the forest before?' Pips shouted to Stump over the roar of his staghorn beetle.

'Na! We stick to what we know. Except for a blast into FernGully every now and again, we hang out round here. This is our territory.'

'It doesn't smell too good,' said Sandy, holding his nose.

'That's because everyone's scared of water around here,' said Pips. 'Stump makes sure it never rains in Stoney Creek!'

'Go on with ya!' bellowed Stump. 'We got water. What do ya think we drink with our beetle juice?' He pulled a mouldy container out of his filthy snakeskin boot and shoved it under Pips' nose. 'Wanna try some?'

Pips shuddered. 'No way, I don't touch that stuff.'

'Helps ya see in the dark,' roared Stump, guzzling from the container then speeding off ahead of them.

They crossed the creek at Lyrebird Lookout, where Crysta often came to sing with the birds. But tonight there was no sign of her.

Next Pips led them through the Valley of Echoes.

'This place is great!' said Sandy, clapping his hands and listening for the echo. 'We should play out here. It would give our music a different buzz.'

'Yep, and wake up the whole valley!' said Wilkea, laughing.

Pips remembered the last time he and Crysta had flown out here. They'd been caught in a heavy rainstorm and had found shelter in the roots of a tree, which turned out to be the home of a family of marsupial mice. The mice invited them to dinner, and they stayed in their warm burrow until the storm had passed. Pips checked out the burrow, but now it was empty.

They kept flying, but when there was still no sign of Crysta at Fallen Tree Gap, Pips began to feel really worried. This was as far as any of them had ever come.

'Could she be at the Blue Grotto?' Sandy asked.

'No way!' said Pips. Then relaxing a little, he grinned. 'I asked her to go there with me the other day, and she really got into a flap. Let's try Possumwood. Baby possums seem to be the love of her life at the moment.'

They changed course and flew low over the forest floor, weaving and twisting around the trees. The moon was no longer overhead and the forest was dark.

'Things don't seem right,' Pips said to Sandy. 'I've got a bad feeling about all this. She's never stayed away from home this long before.'

Sandy told him not to worry, they all knew Crysta could look after herself better than most. But the Beetle Boys couldn't resist teasing Pips.

'Bet she got eaten by a falcon,' said Bark.

'Or a goanna,' said Twigs, giggling.

Eventually Stump decided he was hungry and wanted to rest. Wilkea was only too happy to get off Knot's beetle and stretch his legs. But when they parked, they were surpised to see that all the foliage in the area was dead.

'No chance of a feed around here,' grumbled Stump.

'What could have caused it, Wil?' asked Sandy.

'Don't know,' Wilkea replied, shaking his head. 'But I certainly hope we don't meet up with whatever it was!'

'Look over here!' shouted Knot. 'This old dragon

has taken a nosedive.'

Pips looked at the stiff body of the angle-headed dragon and was shocked to see that it was Draggs. 'I know this little dragon. He's a friend of Crysta's.'

'There's more bods over here,' grunted Stump, pointing to a gecko, a land mullet and a skink lying dead against a blackened tree trunk.

'Let's get out of here,' whimpered Bark, kick-starting his beetle.

But Draggs was still breathing, and Pips refused to leave until they'd helped him. He found a copper-coloured brushtail possum who happily agreed to help them lift Draggs up into his tree.

'There's a hollow in the trunk up here. Fixed up with leaves, it will be comfortable,' said the possum. 'I'll keep an eye on him. He can't stay down on the ground. There's a black mist swirling around that kills everything it touches.'

'So we noticed,' said Stump.

With the possum's help they pulled Draggs up the tree and laid him in the hollow.

'I wish Crysta was here,' said Pips. 'She'd know what to do for him.'

'I'll stay,' said Wilkea. 'I watched how Crysta healed the bat. I can look after him.'

'Then I'll stay, too,' volunteered Sandy. 'I can fetch water from the creek. Pips, you keep looking for Crysta. Don't worry about us, we'll get back in the morning.'

'It won't be long before first light,' said Pips. 'I only hope Crysta and the bat have survived better than Draggs.'

Leaving Wilkea and Sandy to nurse the little dragon, Pips and the Beetle Boys flew off.

'This is a waste of time,' grumbled Bark.

'Yeah, she's probably found another boyfriend,' sneered Twigs.

Pips ignored their remarks and called out Crysta's name over and over again.

As the first light of morning appeared, they found the creek and followed it upstream. Pips was surprised to see little rainbows glistening on the water. It looked as though someone had shredded a rainbow and scattered it about, but he didn't have time to think about it, because Twigs discovered something even more unusual.

A shiny, flat yellow object was floating downstream towards them. They all skidded to a halt above it. None of them had ever seen anything like it before. It looked like a flat piece of wood, only it wasn't the colour of wood and it had perfectly symmetrical edges. Pips cautiously reached down and touched its shiny surface.

'Whatever it is, it's dead,' he whispered. 'We've got to get this back to FernGully. This could have something to do with Crysta's disappearance.'

Stump ordered Bark and Twigs to help him find a way to haul it back to FernGully. He ordered Knot to keep searching for Crysta with Pips. 'And ya never know,' he sniffed, 'if ya keeps ya eyes open, ya might find some other good stuff floatin' around.'

14

THE WEB OF LIFE

hat morning, Crysta knew something was wrong even before she opened her eyes. The fungus platform was moving underneath her in short sharp bursts. Each movement sent a dull throbbing pain through her body.

When she looked over the edge of the platform, she saw Zak standing at the foot of the tree, hammering away at the trunk. She flew down and asked him what he was doing. He proudly told her he was carving her name in the trunk.

'But you mustn't do that!' she cried. 'You're hurting it! Can't you feel its pain?'

Zak didn't know what she was talking about, so Crysta placed his hand on the trunk and told him to feel for himself. Batty, who was hanging overhead, told her that humans were numb from the brain down and couldn't feel anything.

'Are you trying to tell me you can actually *feel* the

life of this tree through the palm of your hand?' Zak asked.

'Of course!' she said.

'Then tell me how!'

'Well, the same way I feel my own nose, or the tip of my toes. I feel it because it's a part of me.'

'Well, it isn't a part of me,' Zak said. 'I think you're forgetting that I'm human. I'm not endowed with fairy magic.'

'Told you he was a trunk-head,' bleeped Batty.

Crysta told Zak that it had nothing to do with being a fairy. It had to do with life—didn't he know that everything living was part of everything else?

Zak just laughed. 'Well, *I'm* certainly not part of a tree!'

Crysta gently shook the branch of a nearby walking stick palm and showed him what she meant. As the tree swayed, a baby bird flapped out of it, dropping the seed it was eating.

'You see, that's what happens when something is disturbed. It affects something else. Come on, I'll show you around the forest.' Holding his hand, she pulled him behind her. She was proud of her forest, and she wanted him to enjoy it as much as she did.

'See this flowering brush box?' She pointed to a huge shady tree that was ringing with the sound of crimson rosellas. 'If that one single tree died, it would affect us all. No more seeds, no more flowers, no more pollen, no more bees, no more birds. And see this spider web?' she asked, lightly bouncing up and down on it. 'If I break one strand, the whole web collapses. All of life is like this web. We're all connected by a very special magic.'

'How about you and me?' Zak grinned as he lifted

her down from the web.

'We're a part of everything, too,' she said, slipping away from him.

A wanderer butterfly offered Zak a lift and he chased Crysta through the trees, clinging to its back. The deeper Zak travelled into the forest, the more completely he fell under its spell.

Batty flapped along behind them, wishing loudly that Zak would disappear out of their lives. 'I feel the gloom of doom,' he muttered unhappily.

When Crysta stopped to rest by the creek, Zak discovered a set of bright red toadstools and decided they would make a great drum kit. He began to rap out a rhythm. He listened to the frogs croak and kept in time with them. A blue freshwater crayfish scrambled out of the creek and joined in, playing percussion with its massive front pincers. Crysta began to dance to their beat: slowly at first, then faster and faster she twirled.

'There are worlds within worlds,' she half-sang, laughing as she danced. 'If the web of life connects me and you then you must be magic like I am too.'

Zak laughed at her song, then he drummed faster. More forest creatures appeared along the banks of the creek, watching.

'He's fallen in fairy love,' whispered an orange and black ladybird to a jewel beetle.

'Could be worse,' the jewel beetle replied. 'He could have fallen in the creek.'

Not even a sudden shower of rain, or Batty's rude remarks, dampened their happy mood.

'The trees make a lot of rain,' explained Crysta, standing beside Zak under the broad leaves of an umbrella tree. 'And the rain makes everything grow.

Without the rain, there wouldn't be a rainforest, and if there wasn't a rainforest none of us would be here.'

While they waited for the rain to ease, Zak produced a squashed, half-eaten sandwich he'd been saving. Removing the plastic wrapper, he offered Crysta a bite.

'Do fairies ever eat?' he asked.

'Yes, often!' she said, picking up the plastic and examining it closely. She stuffed it into her pouch for safekeeping. She bit into Zak's sandwich, but quickly spat it out.

'That's horrible!'

'How about you, Batman?' Zak shouted to Batty, who was hanging sadly from the top branches of the umbrella tree. Batty looked suspiciously at the sandwich.

'Why? Is it laced with poison?'

'No, it's not,' said Zak, annoyed that Batty still refused to be friendly.

'Are you sure?' screeched Batty.

'I'm positive,' yelled Zak.

'Only fools are positive.'

'Are you sure?'

'I'm positive,' said Batty before he realised what he'd said.

Crysta laughed at Batty, but she wished he wasn't so unhappy. She couldn't imagine why he'd taken such an instant dislike to Zak.

When the rain eased to a light drizzle, they started walking. A red-necked pademelon followed them for some way, then shyly asked if they'd like a lift.

Crysta was thrilled to be offered such a good ride and she helped Zak climb into the pademelon's pouch.

'Short-circuit side-effects! Don't put *that* in your pouch!' yelled Batty. But the pademelon ignored him.

It was well past noon when the pademelon stopped and let Zak out of her pouch. 'This is as far as I'm going,' she said apologetically. 'I'm visiting my cousin Mel here at Myrtle Beech Falls.'

'It's not far to FernGully from here,' said Crysta, thanking her.

'Look at this!' called Zak, dragging a dried black bean pod towards Crysta. 'I've found us a canoe.'

He pushed the pod into the water and jumped into it, steering it with a miniature palm frond. 'Come on, it's my turn to take you on a ride you won't forget.'

Crysta hovered overhead then lowered herself into the canoe. She sat in the bow facing Zak as they rode the rapids.

When the water calmed, they drifted lazily with the current, past stream lilies and water gums, and under the fronds of elegant bangalow palms. A squadron of rainbow lorikeets darted out of the trees and followed the canoe down the creek. They skimmed over the water, twisting and turning without breaking ranks.

Crysta called to Batty to keep up with them, but for the first time in their long journey he didn't reply to her call.

'You see, there's more to life than flying,' Zak said, grinning, pleased to be in control of their journey for the first time.

The sudden roar of a waterfall took Zak completely by surprise. He didn't have a chance to stop the canoe before it shot straight over the edge.

15

ZAK MEETS THE FERNGULLY MOB

Being light as a feather, Crysta was left floating in the air when the canoe dropped out from under her. At first she didn't know what had happened to them, until she saw Zak hurtling down the falls.

As she flew down to rescue him, the Beetle Boys suddenly darted in front of her and Stump scooped Zak up before he hit the bottom. He threw him onto the back of his beetle like a drowned mosquito and buzzed off at top speed.

Crysta shouted to them to be careful of Zak because he was a human, but this news only made Stump more excited.

'A *hooman*!?! Wahoo!! Yabblesheeb!!' he bellowed, disappearing through the trees.

'Hey, come back!' shouted Crysta, chasing after him. 'That's *my* human!'

She chased them through the trees towards the

heart of FernGully, shooting through narrow openings in vines and zipping through dense foliage. Then suddenly Batty appeared and flapped across Stump's flight path, and they crashed straight into one another.

Zak was thrown off Stump's beetle and hurtled through the air, landing with a thump in the roots of *Old Hi Rise*.

Fairies and elves scattered in fright as this strange new creature fell from the sky. But when everyone discovered that Crysta was home, they ran from their hiding places to greet her.

'Welcome back, sugar-face,' screeched Blackbeak from his perch. 'What have you brought back with you this time?'

Crysta's mother flew to her. 'Thank goodness you're home!' she sobbed.

Lily and Fern dashed out of *Old Hi Rise* to see what had happened to their sister. 'Look at her torn clothes,' said Fern. 'She must have gone through something terrible.'

Batty had also crashed into *Old Hi Rise*, but no-one was taking any notice of him.

'Nobody cares about *me*,' he bleeped sadly, disentangling his wings from a hanging vine. 'Another perfect landing. No worries. Just a few bruises. Shock therapy. She'll be right. No cause for alarm.'

'I care, Batman,' groaned Zak, standing up and limping over to where Batty lay in a twisted heap.

'You?' Batty bleeped nervously. 'Are you sure?'

Zak grinned. 'I'm positive.'

'But only fools are positive,' muttered Batty.

'Are you sure?' asked Zak.

But before Batty could answer, Zak was whisked off by Crysta and led past a long row of fairies to the Elfin Elders.

'And just what have we here?' asked Ash, looking closely at Zak.

Just then Pips flew through the trees with Knot buzzing behind him. They both looked exhausted.

'Crysta! We've been looking everywhere for you. Where on earth have you been?' he said, flying down beside her.

'Pips, you won't believe what I've found,' she said, pointing to Zak.

But Pips was not impressed, and said to her angrily, 'Is that all you've got to say? I've been out all night and you want to show me some weird creature!'

'This weird creature happens to be a human,' Crysta replied coldly.

Pips stood in front of Zak then fluttered off the ground so he was head and shoulders above him. 'Kinda small, isn't he?'

Then Stump and Twig turned up with Mel the pademelon. Only Mel wasn't carrying Paddy in her pouch as she hopped towards them. Instead, there was a hard, shiny and rock-like object sticking out of it.

Ash asked Mel to explain what she'd brought home. Mel said she didn't know, but she was only too happy to off-load it. It wasn't as big as Paddy, but it wasn't as soft, either. She set it against a tree trunk then quickly hopped away.

'It's simple, really,' said Pips, walking towards it and tapping its shiny surface. 'It's hard like stone, yet hollow. And it has this little vine shooting out of the side.'

Zak pushed past him. 'Hey, that's my Walkman!'

'I found it, so I'll explain it!' said Pips, silencing Zak with an icy stare.

'Then tell us what it is.'

'Well, it's obviously ... obviously ... a ...' Pips stuttered.

Zak ignored him and climbed up onto his Walkman. He looked down at the sea of puzzled faces turned towards him, and stamped on the play button. The loud roar of music that blasted out of the headphones sent everyone diving for cover.

'It's alive,' cried Ash, peeping out from behind a tree.

'And it's noisy,' said Jips, peering over his shoulder.

Zak tried to convince them it was quite harmless. 'It's only a recording of music,' he explained.

'I don't know what a recording is, but I know what music is, and that is *not* music!' said Ash firmly.

'It sounds good to me,' said Crysta, twirling in time to the beat.

'It's great to dance to!' Fern giggled, fluttering and twisting beside her sister.

Soon, all the young fairies and elves were dancing, even the babies. Then everyone joined in, dancing or singing or flapping along in time to the music.

Caught up in the happy mood, even Jips and Ash tapped their toes. Rose Myrtle watched her fairy ballerinas dance like she'd never seen them dance before. She wasn't sure whether to laugh or cry.

Zak jumped behind a set of fungi drums and played along. Pips pulled out his flute and challenged him with complicated riffs. The dancing became wilder and the singing louder as Pips and Zak competed with one another over the song blasting out of Zak's stereo. Then Zak suddenly stopped drumming and started to dance with Crysta. Imitating his every move, Crysta wiggled her hips and waved her arms. Faster and faster she danced, until she was a blur against the trees.

Pips glowed with jealousy and he decided he didn't like Zak. Crysta was *his* best friend, and now this outsider had bewitched her. Pips knew Zak meant trouble, he could feel it in the tips of his wings. Before the song ended, Pips had decided on a plan of action to teach Zak a lesson he wouldn't forget. He grinned mischievously to himself as he thought about it.

When the music and dancing finally stopped, Pips told Zak that he and the Beetle Boys wanted to show him the *real* FernGully. Zak knew that, like Batty, Pips had taken an instant dislike to him. So he accepted what he knew to be a challenge, to prove to Pips and the rough-looking Beetle Boys that he was up to anything they could dish out. But he certainly wasn't prepared for what they had in mind.

They gave him Stump's beetle, Stinger, to ride. Stinger turned out to be a bad-tempered bug with a mind of his own, who tried to sting him every chance he could. When Zac heard them discussing where to fly, and they talked about places called Eagles' Window and Thunder Falls, he knew he was in for a bad time. He could ride, but he'd never been on the back of a beetle before, and to make it worse, once they were airborne Stinger kept flying upside down through prickly vines.

When Pips raced a kingfisher along the creek,

Stinger decided to join in the chase. Up Thunder Falls they flew, almost drowning in the spray. Down the falls they plummeted, chasing one another dangerously.

Stinger was in a frenzy of excitement. He overtook the other beetles and raced after the kingfisher, which seemed to be flying at supersonic speed. Zak closed his eyes and held his breath when Stinger gained height on the bird and dived towards a rocky bank of the creek.

'Go, Stinger!' yelled Stump from the back of Twig's beetle. 'He beat ya, King. Ya been beaten by a hooman!'

'It was only luck,' said Pips disdainfully. 'Let's see how he handles Crawling Rock.'

The Beetle Boys agreed that Crawling Rock would certainly test Zak. It was a huge rock in the middle of the creek which was crawling with tiny leeches.

16
TROUBLE IN PARADISE

Crysta was worried when she heard that Pips and the Beetle Boys had taken Zak for a ride around FernGully. She raced after them, hoping she'd find Zak before he was in too much trouble. She knew Black Rock Cutting or Thunder Falls were the most likely places to find them, so she took off down the creek in that direction.

But before she'd gone very far, she saw Magi Lune floating ahead of her. Crysta wondered what had brought Magi out of her beech tree forest, and she was surprised to see her weighed down with a heavy basket. Crysta couldn't wait to tell Magi everything that had happened since she'd last seen her, but when she caught up to her at Fossil Bend, the old fairy didn't give her a chance to say anything.

'Good, you're turning up whenever I need you these days. Don't tell me you're becoming responsible, Crysta!'

'Well, I was really looking for Pips and the Beetle Boys,' Crysta confessed.

'The point is, you are with me now. How you got here really isn't important.' Magi handed Crysta her basket. 'I need your help. Paddy is ill. Sandy and Wilkea brought in an angle-headed dragon earlier this morning. I'm doing what I can, but until I know the cause of the sickness, it's hard to treat.'

'But they'll be all right, won't they?'

'I certainly hope so,' said Magi, hurrying to collect fungi spore and flower pollen, which she asked Crysta to carry in her pouch.

'I need to find a remedy for this sickness. There is a poison in the wind, and the rain is starting to burn. I've never encountered anything like it before.'

Magi hurried ahead of Crysta and swept into the beech tree forest. When they arrived at her home, Crysta was shocked to see Ock and Rock standing watch over five motionless little bodies. Her friends! They looked seriously ill.

Slider was propped up against the trunk of the tree. Beside him lay Draggs, Paddy and a yellow-breasted robin called Silky. A baby echidna and a snake were lying next to them.

'What happened?' she asked, rushing up to Slider.

'I'm all right, Crysta,' he whimpered. 'It's Paddy I'm worried about. Mel left him with me at Myrtle Falls while she carried a load back in her pouch for Stump. I stayed awake to help out. If Paddy dies, I'll never forgive myself!'

'Paddy *isn't* going to die! Did he eat any "go-to-sleep-leaves"?'

'No, he just said he felt dizzy and got weaker every hop. I pushed him back here and then he collapsed.'

Slider's soft brown eyes were wide with concern. 'We ran into Silky along the way, and she said she felt sick too. I didn't know where you were, so I brought them here.'

'You did the right thing, Slider. Lucky for them you were around.'

'Well, at least we know one thing,' said Magi, plucking a tiny feather from Silky's wing and hurrying inside her house. 'They were all outside FernGully when they fell sick.'

'But what would make them this sick?' Crysta asked, following Magi inside and watching while Magi prepared a mixture of herbs.

'Silky's feather shows she's been exposed to a very strong poison,' Magi replied, nodding towards the feather she'd placed beside her diamond-shaped crystal. 'It can only be Hexxus. I feel his energy getting stronger. What I can't work out is how Hexxus can be growing so fast. For now, I can reverse the effects of his poison, but if he gets any stronger, this whole forest is in great danger.'

Crysta was shocked. 'But you told me there wasn't a force in nature that could release Hexxus!'

'I said there wasn't a *natural* force that could release him. There's something most *un*natural about all this,' she said, unfurling a bark scroll and concentrating on the symbols engraved on it. She sighed, looking up at Crysta. 'I'm too old for this. To reverse the power of Hexxus, so much energy is needed.'

'But surely you can stop him?'

'Alone, my power is limited. When I defeated Hexxus before, I was young and strong and I had the support of the whole forest behind me. Things are very different now.'

Magi went outside and attended to the sick animals. She gave each of them a mouthful of the creamy green mixture she'd prepared. While she fed them she summoned her healing powers through the tips of her fingers: one by one, the animals stirred and opened their eyes.

'Slider, where are you?' cried Paddy, sitting up and rubbing his eyes.

'I'm right here, Paddy,' said Slider, scampering towards him.

Silky fluffed out her feathers. 'Hello, Crysta,' she chirped. 'I had a horrible dream.'

The python suddenly hissed and slithered silently away. The echidna stretched her quills and asked shyly, 'What happened to me?'

Only Draggs remained motionless. Nothing Magi could do had any effect on the angle-headed dragon.

'He's in shock,' said Magi. 'I'll keep him here with me. Crysta, you and Slider see Silky, Treena and Paddy home as quickly as you can. And tomorrow I want you to collect some crystals from the Blue Grotto. I'll need to prepare a lot of remedies in case this poison spreads.'

'Of course,' Crysta said, willing to do anything the old fairy said.

'Better not say anything about this trouble for the moment. We don't want everyone to panic,' Magi said, hurrying Crysta out of the beech tree circle.

Crysta set off home feeling very confused. As she trekked through the forest beside the baby echidna, the sun cast its long afternoon shadows around them; she hoped she'd get back to *Old Hi Rise* before dark. No-one would give Treena a lift, because her spikes were too prickly, and that slowed them down.

Crysta wished she'd told Magi about Zak and the Silent Forest, but she smiled to herself when she thought how surprised Magi would be tomorrow. She made up her mind to take Zak with her to the Blue Grotto, then after that, on to Magi Lune's.

When she led her young team into Sleepy Hollow, Slider said he'd keep an eye on Treena while Crysta hurried ahead of them to check on Little Hoop. But when she saw Little Hoop, she knew there was something dreadfully wrong. The tree had grown very tall—it was already taller than any other tree in Sleepy Hollow—but it was as thin as a twig. Crysta knew at a glance that it was about to topple over.

'Oh, Little Hoop! I know I wanted you to be the tallest tree in the forest, but not like this!'

Stoneface looked grim, with not a trace of a smile on his rugged face.

'Stoneface, tell me what to do.'

But he didn't say anything, he just stared in stony silence. Crysta felt dreadful as she knelt beside Little Hoop, closed her eyes and touched its skinny trunk.

'I know I've done something wrong, and I'm really sorry, Little Hoop, please forgive me. I take back what I said. I don't care how tall you grow. I just want you to be the *strongest* tree in the forest.'

When she opened her eyes, she thought she heard a sigh of relief from Little Hoop. When she turned to Stoneface she thought she saw a smile.

'Wow, you've got to be careful what you say around here,' she said, brushing fallen leaves off the top of the rock's moss-covered head. 'No wonder you keep your mouth shut!'

She waved goodbye to them both, promising to

return tomorrow, and caught up to the others as they were crossing the creek at Python Rock. Treena echidna's mother was waiting for her.

'Oh, thank you, Crysta!' she said. 'I've been worried sick! Treena is at that age where she wanders off by herself all the time. This time she's been away since new moon.'

Without Treena slowing them down, they covered the distance from Python Rock to *Old Hi Rise* quickly. Paddy darted through the forest in sudden bursts of speed, at times dashing so fast that Slider had trouble keeping up with him. When Paddy found his mother, he squealed with delight and scrambled headfirst into her pouch. Silky flew off to her nest in a nearby tangle of lawyer vines.

Crysta and Slider arrived at *Old Hi Rise* as the sun was setting. Crysta found Zak sitting on a branch beside Blackbeak. Her mother was fussing over him, healing cuts and bruises on his arms and legs. Batty was hanging directly above, watching Zak suspiciously.

'This poor young thing is all roughed up,' said her mother. 'What's wrong with Pips? He should know better than to take a newcomer to Crawling Rock. It's the most dangerous part of the forest.'

'Don't worry about me, I'm okay.' Zak grinned, and made a place on the branch for Crysta to sit beside him. 'But I don't think your boyfriend likes me too much.'

'He's *not* my boyfriend,' Crysta muttered, glowing in the twilight.

'I've made Zak a bed in the spare hollow above us,' said her mother, before disappearing inside the tree.

'Oh, no!' bleeped Batty. 'Hang a fang, Crystabellis. Don't take *that* inside your home. You'll be semi-quavered!'

'Stop flapping your beak,' squawked Blackbeak. 'If he's a mate of Crysta's, he must be okay.'

'We've had quite enough excitement for one day,' screeched Queenie, from her staghorn nest below them. 'It's time to settle down.'

'I agree,' yawned Crysta. 'Come on, Zak, I'll show you where you can sleep.'

'Oh, no, no, no, no, NO!' bleeped Batty, covering his head with his wings as Zak disappeared through the fungus doorway with Crysta.

Al, a lyrebird, was mimicking all the sounds.

17

THE BLUE GROTTO

Crysta woke up late the next morning, and when she saw Zak, he was sitting at the round table in their eating hollow, surrounded by her family. Her sisters seemed very interested in him.

'You didn't tell me you had two such stunning sisters,' he said, making way for her at the table and offering her a bowl of berries soaked in melted honey dew.

'I'm glad they like you so much. I only wish Pips and Batty felt the same way.'

'Crysta, Zak's been telling us about a place called *skool*,' said Fern. 'It sounds so funny!'

'Sounds like a good idea to me,' replied Grandfather Ash, gulping down a stemful of fruit nectar. 'Especially the bit about learning. I wish there was more learning and less skylarking around this forest.'

'Crysta, there's been trouble in the forest

overnight,' said her mother, not wishing to rake over old arguments. 'I'm going out to Possumwood, there's something out there making the babies sick.'

'We'll meet you out there after dance class,' said Fern, leaping up from the table. 'Come on, Lily, or we'll be late again and Myrtle the turtle will be furious.'

'I'm going to help with repairs to the canopy,' said Ash, getting up from the table and pulling on his waistcoat. 'Whole sections of the forest are reporting damage of some sort, and there wasn't a storm last night! It's very strange.'

Crysta told them she was taking Zak to the Blue Grotto to collect some crystals and herbs that might help the animals. She hurried Zak outside and showed him an easy way to climb down *Old Hi Rise*. While he was slowly and carefully climbing down, she told him about her friend the strangler fig.

'Did you know that this tree grows down, instead of up? That makes it pretty special, doesn't it? First of all, a seed is dropped in a fork or a branch of a tree, and this seed then has to send out a long, thin runner to the ground. When it hits the ground it branches out and forms a hollow trunk of roots around the tree. It's great to live in, because the trunk is so thick, and yet there's a hollow up the centre, so it's always cool and airy. And—' she grinned at Zak 'there's fruit on this tree most of the year, that's why so many birds live in it.'

Once on solid ground again, Zak looked up and admired the towering tree. He saw that it was decorated with hundreds of staghorn ferns and climbing orchids.

'Okay, you've convinced me it's special,' he said.

'So what's next?'

Crysta told him they were going to the Blue Grotto but, to her surprise, he wasn't at all pleased.

'But I thought we were going to find this Magi character. Remember your promise to unshrink me?'

'Oh Zak, aren't you having a good time? What's wrong?'

'What's wrong? What's wrong is I'm suddenly knee-high to a grasshopper, which may seem fine to you, but believe me, it's very weird.'

Crysta tried to hide her disappointment.

'It's just that I thought you might want to stay here for a while.'

Blackbeak flew down to join them, and Crysta asked him if he'd give them a lift to the Blue Grotto then fly them to Magi Lune's. Blackbeak was only too happy to oblige, and soon they were being ferried through the trees on his back.

Like Zak, Blackbeak was an outsider. Long ago he'd arrived in FernGully from another rainforest, and stayed. He was blind in one eye and had a stump of a leg, but he would never talk about where he'd come from or how he'd received his battle scars.

As they flew towards the Blue Grotto, the trees grew closer together and soon they were flying through leafy archways of interlocking palms and tree ferns. When they reached the Blue Grotto, Blackbeak said he'd be back to collect them after he'd visited some cockatoo friends nearby.

It was a hot steamy morning, and Zak was happy to see they'd stopped at a perfect place to swim— above the entrance to the Blue Grotto was a series of crystal-clear pools. He pulled off his sneakers and tee-shirt and dived into the clear sparkling water.

Crysta dived gracefully after him, then surfaced next to him riding the tail of a young platypus. She laughed at his surprise and beckoned him to follow her towards an underwater cave.

Inside the cave it was very quiet. The walls glowed with a soft blue light. Crysta filled her pouch with tiny crystals she chipped from the rocks. When her pouch was full, she led Zak around the slippery rocks to a deep chasm which separated them from more underwater caves.

'We have to cross this to get into the Blue Grotto,' she said, trying not to smile.

Zak said there was no way he was going to risk his life by plunging into it, but Crysta laughed.

'It's an illusion, silly! It only looks deep because of the reflection of the blue rocks above it. But it's really shallow.' She waded through it to show him where another series of pools glistened in the eerie blue light. Bending over one of them, Crysta stirred the water and created a spinning top with it. She whisked it out of the water and threw it to Zak, but when he caught it the bubble burst, and he was drenched.

'You'll keep!' he shouted, watching her dance away from him, across the top of the shallow underground pools. But he found there was no way *he* could walk on top of the water. Crysta copied his clumsy attempts, and they laughed and splashed around from one pool to the next. Then she led him to the one pool she knew was really deep. Tiptoeing across the top of it, she beckoned him to follow. He stepped into it and disappeared!

She dived in to rescue him, but now it was her turn to be surprised—Zak grabbed her around the waist, and surfaced holding her high above his head.

'Got you now!' he cried. But, to his amazement, she disappeared in a burst of shimmering light. All that was left was the glowing outline of her body hanging in the air above his head. She'd tricked him again! He turned, and saw her disappear into a cave and he followed her.

The cave was lit by millions of glow-worms. Crysta smiled when she heard Zak catch his breath at the sight of them, for it was exactly the reaction she'd hoped for. The Blue Grotto was a very special place. She looked at Zak in the twinkling light, and was glad she'd brought him here.

They left a sparkling phosphorescent trail behind them as they swam slowly into the centre of the cave. Zak floated on his back, looking up at the glow-worm ceiling. He felt as though he was in heaven, with a million stars shining down on him.

Crysta floated in the air above him, glowing with her own dazzling beauty among the twinkling lights. As he watched her, he knew that she'd touched his heart forever. He knew he would never forget this moment.

As if sensing this, Crysta dived into the water and surfaced to face him. She held out her hands towards him and when he touched them she locked their fingers together.

Zak felt lighter than air. Without thinking, he leant forward and kissed her.

Crysta looked stunned when they parted, but Zak was even more stunned when he discovered they were no longer in the water, but hanging motionless in the air, suspended under the twinkling lights of the glow-worm cavern.

'What's happening?' he whispered.

'What do you mean?' she asked, looking at him tenderly.

He nodded towards the water below. 'We're hanging in space, in case you haven't noticed.'

Crysta smiled, then loosened her hands. They floated slowly back into the water.

'My body feels so light!' *he* said.

'That's because it is. That's the magic of fairy love. We share the same feelings now.'

She swam back towards the narrow opening to the cave. She told him they shouldn't stay for too long, because the magic in the Blue Grotto was so strong it could entice them to stay forever. Zak said he wouldn't mind, but Crysta insisted that they leave.

'I thought you wanted to see Magi Lune and get unshrunk,' she said, when they finally clambered onto the rocks below Crystal Falls.

'Later. You were right. I do like it here.'

'No, I promised. I cast a spell, and shrank you by mistake. Such a spell must be reversed.'

She sat beside him on the rocks, drying her wings. They were both so happy that they didn't see the tell-tale signs of Hexxus all around them. They didn't know Hexxus had followed them to Crystal Falls, poisoning everything in his path.

18
BETRAYED!

hen Blackbeak didn't turn up, Crysta said she was going to fly to Magi Lune's, because she knew Magi was waiting for the crystals she'd collected.

Zak said he'd wait for Blackbeak. He was only too happy to stay and dry off in the sun. But after a while it was too hot, and he climbed onto the bank of the creek and lay beneath a shady tree.

As soon as he lay down, he felt sick. At first it was a dizziness, but when he leant back against the tree, he felt a sharp pain. He looked at the tree more closely, and saw that it was dying before his eyes! And, strangely, he felt as though a part of him was dying too...

He jumped back into the creek, but when he looked down at his feet, he saw he was standing in a pool of oil. A steady rivulet of dark oil was trickling over the falls and collecting in the crystal-clear pools below. While he stared at the waterfall, Crysta's platypus friend clambered up the bank with her family. They, too, were covered in oil.

Zak ran along the bank of the creek, calling out to Crysta. He didn't know if she could hear him, but he had to do something to warn her about this danger!

As she flew through the forest, Crysta did hear his warning. It sent a violent shiver right through her. She stopped flying, her body alert and tense with fear. 'The sickness! Oh no, I hope I haven't caught it,' she thought, dropping down into Sleepy Hollow to rest for a moment.

It was just as well she did drop into Sleepy Hollow, because Little Hoop was in trouble too. The pine tree had completely changed shape. It was no longer tall, but very short, more like a squashed bush than a tree, its needles hanging in limp clusters at the top of its strong, stubby branches. It looked so sad that Crysta felt like crying. When she looked at Stoneface, he didn't look any happier. She touched Little Hoop's needles.

'Little Hoop, I don't know what's happened. But if it's something I've said, then I'm truly sorry. I don't care what you look like. I just want you to be happy.'

She only wished there was something she could say to Stoneface that might make him feel better. She hated seeing her friends like this, and she knew she had to find Magi Lune fast. There were too many unexplained things happening in the forest. A deep, awful fear began to curl its cold fingers around her heart.

She left Little Hoop and Stoneface and flew at top speed towards the Antarctic beech trees and Magi Lune. She didn't slow down until she saw Ock and

Rock. She fluttered past the big birds and into Magi's house. But although the door was wide open, Magi wasn't there. She called Magi's name over and over again, but there was no reply. Then she noticed a vibrant green path twisting through the trees. She knew it had to be Magi's trail, so she followed it.

Like the trees and flowers around her, she immediately felt better when she was close to Magi Lune. However, the further she flew, she noticed a marked contrast in the trees. In areas where Magi hadn't been the foliage was dying. Leaves hung limply, as if in mourning for the dead plants and flowers shrivelled up around them. She saw a glimmer of sunshine ahead and knew Magi must be close by.

Crysta found Magi sitting on an outstretched branch of a fallen tree. She looked exhausted. Her energy field was reduced to a pale glow and her petalled robes, usually so fresh and bright, were wilted and soiled.

'Oh, Magi!' she cried, rushing towards her. 'Magi...what's wrong?'

Magi didn't answer. She stared at the tree stump in front of her. It was absolutely flat, as if it had been cut through in one mighty blow. When Crysta touched its smooth surface, she couldn't feel any life in it.

'Magi, you can heal it, can't you?'

'No. I can't heal it...and I can't stop it,' said Magi sadly.

'But I know what did this!' said Crysta, suddenly remembering what she'd seen in the silent forest. 'Magi, I know what caused this. It's a monster the humans fight. It's called a *masheen*. Zak can stop it.

He makes red marks that protect the trees.'

She flew around the tree stump, then stopped and stared. There, quite clearly, were the remains of a red mark. When she looked at other fallen trees, she saw that they were also marked. In that terrible moment she realised that these red marks were the marks of death.

'But Zak said . . . Zak told me the trees were safe.'

Deep in thought, Magi still didn't reply, so Crysta flew towards the canopy. As she spiralled upwards, she knew there was something dreadfully wrong. When Magi didn't call her back, not even when she flew beyond the treetops and out into the open sky, she knew the trouble was serious.

She hovered, waiting until her eyes adjusted to the glare, then forced herself to stare at the horror below. Instead of dense forest, all that was left was a vast plain of tree stumps stretching to the horizon. The huge yellow monster she'd glimpsed in the silent forest growled up at her from the front line of devastation.

Magi Lune silently floated up beside her, and they looked down at the scene together.

'It's the monster,' Crysta sobbed, pointing at the idling machine. 'And more humans!'

They watched two men walk towards the machine and climb inside. The machine suddenly roared to life, belching a thick cloud of dark smoke as it lurched forward and sliced through a whole row of trees. Crysta doubled up in pain as the trees fell.

'Humans,' she sobbed. 'Humans are killing our forest.'

'Yes,' said Magi. 'But more than humans. Their destructive ways have unleashed Hexxus.'

Crysta looked up as a dark billowing cloud rolled towards them. From its depths an evil face leered at them. It blew a gust of putrid air around them. Its fiery eyes glowed yellow with anger when it saw Magi Lune.

'Humans have unearthed our old enemy, and he's getting bigger every day,' said Magi, quickly dropping below the canopy. 'The humans don't even know what they've done. Hexxus has attached himself to their poisonous machine. I don't think they know he's there. They don't realise that Hexxus will kill them too.'

Magi Lune led Crysta back into the forest. 'We must tell the Elders at once,' she said firmly.

Zak was already waiting for Crysta at *Old Hi Rise*; Blackbeak had picked him up as he was running along the creek. They'd both been shocked to see so many dead fish floating downstream.

Zak was relieved when he saw Crysta flying towards him. He knew only too well that his friends at the logging camp were responsible for the oil spill. He had to tell her the truth about what was happening at the edge of the forest. But when he called out to her, she just stared at him and flew straight past.

A crowd had gathered around *Old Hi Rise*. Zak noticed the Elfin Elders huddled together, talking among themselves.

'Something is killing our forest!' shouted a voice from the crowd.

'Everyone's getting sick!' cried another.

'What are we going to do?' shouted others.

Zak felt all eyes suddenly turn towards him. He ran to Crysta, but she refused to look at him.

When the Elders saw Magi Lune, they made way for her.

'Can you help us?' said Jips.

'What is it that attacks our forest?' asked Grandfather Ash.

Pushing his way towards them, Zak answered for Magi Lune. '*Humans!*' he said. 'Humans are killing this forest.'

A shocked murmur rolled through the crowd, and the Elfin Elders stared at him.

'Humans are cutting down the trees,' said Zak. 'And I was helping them do it. Batty was right...'

Looking at the puzzled, innocent faces staring at him, he felt a burning shame, but knew he had to continue. 'They're coming this way. You can't stop them. You'll have to... you'll have to leave.'

'Leave FernGully?' echoed the crowd of elves and fairies.

'Where would we go?' whimpered Granny Belladonna.

'There is another way,' said Magi Lune, speaking for the first time. 'Gather everyone in the circle,' she commanded. Then without another word, she floated up and over the crowd and disappeared through the trees. One by one, the fairies and elves followed her. Soon Zak was left alone with Pips and Batty.

Before flying after the others, Pips glared at Zak and said, 'Ever since you arrived, there's been trouble. Go back to your own world, *human!* Go back before you kill us all.'

When Batty saw how genuinely upset Zak was, he felt sorry for him, and offered him a lift to the beech tree forest.

'Hang a fang, you can't stay here alone, even if you are a gloomin' hoomin! But you'll have to walk some of the way, I won't be too popular with you on my back.'

Zak accepted Batty's unexpected offer of friendship and they flapped behind the others in silence. Batty dropped Zak off short of Magi Lune's house. Animals and birds hopped and flew past him, but nobody spoke to him. He stopped to rest beneath a yellow carabeen, but he didn't stay for long, for it was the same sort of tree he'd spent the night in with Crysta, and the thought of how innocent and happy she'd been filled him with a terrible sadness.

The golden light of the setting sun slanted through the mist-shrouded beech trees and Zak slowly followed the birds and animals rushing past him. He heard a sound he hadn't heard before. While he listened to it, it grew louder and louder. At first he thought it was the wind blowing through the trees. But the air was still. Then thousands of twinkling fairies flashed through the forest and gathered at a single point just ahead of him. They filled the trees with their bright flickering light.

Running towards the trees, Zak climbed up a mountainous beech tree root and peered into the fairies' circle of light.

*'State your name, Crysta,' said
Ock importantly.*

19

THE CEREMONY

The fairies sat on branches and vines stretched between the huge trees. Birds and animals gathered around the roots. As evening closed in around them, their light grew brighter. The setting reminded Zak of a candle-lit Christmas service he'd once gone to as a child. He instinctively knew some sort of magic was going to take place here.

As Zak watched them, a single glittering light darted into the circle of ancient trees. Even without seeing her face, he knew it was Crysta.

Then, from the centre of the glowing ring of fairies, Magi Lune appeared, glowing brighter than them all. Everyone was silent as she spoke.

'Since the beginning of time, we have been the guardians of this forest. But we have grown lazy. We have forgotten the magic of nature. The time has come to call on it again.'

She slowly floated down and picked up a tiny seed

from the forest floor. She held the seed up for everyone to see.

'Remember the power that exists within a single seed. That same power also exists within each and every one of us. It is the power of nature. This is the magic we share with all life.'

She began to chant, and the seed glowed.

Zak held his breath as he watched the glowing seed grow brighter than the fairies, until its dazzling light flowed through Magi, into the earth and up through the trees.

Then the singing started. At first it was a low hum, then one by one every tree and plant and tiny flower raised its voice and joined in. The forest was filled with their song, a song without words, but full of pride and hope.

The ancient beech trees sang in their thunderously deep pipe organ tones, while the small plants chimed with crystalline delicacy. And all the while the seed glowed brighter, revealing its hidden power.

The beech trees moved together, closing the gaps that separated them, as if to protect nature's most treasured secret. Zak leapt into the shining circle as the trees twisted shut and plunged the outside forest into darkness.

The fairies fluttered into the air, forming their own circle within the enclosed space. They became a swirling column of light.

But Crysta didn't fly with them. She was mesmerised by the glowing seed. Almost against her will she found herself being drawn closer to it.

Magi smiled, and held out the seed to Crysta.

'Oh, no, Magi, no! I'm not ready.'

'We can't always choose our time, Crysta. *Your*

time is now,' said Magi, closing Crysta's hand around the seed.

From the moment she touched the seed, Crysta felt different. In that moment she knew that, like the tiny seed, she too had a hidden power, a magical strength. As she held the seed, the trees sang louder and the twisting column of fairies spun faster and faster around her.

'Look for the hero inside yourself, Crysta,' Magi Lune was saying in a low voice. 'Look to the good and loving heart inside you and all others. For just as every seed holds the power and magic of creation, so too do you and every other creature in this world. Use this power, Crysta, to unite and make whole. Use it for the good of all.'

As Magi spoke, her body slowly dissolved, until all that was left of her was a tiny, intense point of light.

'Oh Magi, don't leave me...' Crysta cried.

'Old life always has to give way to the new,' whispered Magi. 'Remember, Crysta, this power is generous. It grows when it is shared.'

The sparkling light that Magi had become shone over Crysta. It shone so brightly that it suddenly exploded into a thousand twinkling fragments, and everyone who was gathered in the magic circle was struck by the hurtling sparks. In a daze, Crysta watched one last magic spark drift down to where Zak stood. It seemed to hover above his head, then it landed in the middle of his forehead, illuminating him in a flash of light.

The trees lowered their voices and slowly unwound their trunks. The light from the inner circle now flowed out into the forest, and soon all that was left of Magi's glowing energy was one sparkling point of light in the centre of the Antarctic beech trees. It shone from the seed Crysta held in her hand.

'Magi,' Crysta cried softly, floating down to earth.

'What are we to do, Crysta?' asked Jips, flying towards her.

'What did Magi say?' whispered Elwood.

'That within us all is a magic power that grows when it is shared,' she replied, suddenly realising all eyes were on her; everyone seemed to be looking to her for help.

Remembering what Magi had just told her, she concentrated her energy on the problem they now all faced. Looking around her she noticed something odd. The soft pre-dawn light had crept into the forest, but the forest was deadly quiet. Not a single bird chirped. It was an eerie silence. And then they all heard a deep rumbling sound and the ground began to tremble.

Through the early morning mist another, harsher light emerged, blinding them. Zak ran towards Crysta. 'We've got to get everyone out of here!' he yelled. 'It's the Leveller! It's coming straight towards us.'

Before he could reach her, the canopy was savagely ripped apart and the cruel face of Hexxus leered down at them from above the trees, where he swirled as a furious dark cloud.

'*Fairies*!' he howled, scorching them with his poisonous breath. 'Care for a breath of fresh air?'

'No!' shouted Crysta, tucking the glowing seed into her pouch. Without thinking, she darted towards Hexxus. But with one cruel breath he blew her back against the roots of a beech tree.

'Crysta, move!' yelled Zak, as the trees were lit with a piercing light and the earth crumbled beneath them. An enormous mechanical arm grabbed the ancient beech trees around their trunks and ripped them from the ground. The trees groaned, and their cries filled the forest.

Fairies flew screaming from the scene. Zak ran towards Crysta, who was hovering directly in front of the Leveller.

'Crysta, come on!' he shouted.

'I can't move!' she cried, blinded by the unnatural light.

Zak was suddenly pushed aside by Pips and Batty. 'Go away!' yelled Pips. 'Haven't you done enough, human?' Dragging Crysta out of the path of the Leveller and away from the devastated circle of beech trees, Pips urged her not to look back.

With a heartbreaking scream the rest of the beech trees were uprooted, and Magi's house was smashed in two. All around them the giant trees fell, dragging more of the canopy with them.

'Pips, find Ock and Rock!' screamed Crysta as Hexxus stormed overhead. 'Then meet me back at *Old Hi Rise*. Whatever happens, we've got to save the heart of the forest!'

'Do you like my new toy, fairy?' roared Hexxus, snorting up the Leveller's fumes and puffing himself up grotesquely. 'Let's open up this forest!' he bellowed, scorching the ground with his fiery breath and incinerating a trail of lizards, frogs and beetles who were scurrying through the undergrowth. 'Let's get to the heart of the forest!' he taunted. 'Run, fairies, run!'

Once again Crysta flew towards him. But once

again she was blown back. Hexxus laughed at her foolishness. He reached out with a single black finger and touched the pale fluffy clouds of dawn, turning them into one swirling thundering black cloud, which unleashed a heavy shower of dark acid rain. It burnt and sizzled the leaves of the few trees still standing.

Batty grabbed Crysta and Zak and dived for cover, sheltering them both under his wing. When the burning rain stopped falling, Batty told them to hang on tight and he flapped them back through the forest towards *Old Hi Rise*.

All the forest creatures were now either running or flying towards the strangler fig tree. Terrified voices filled the air and the cries of falling trees almost drowned out the roar of the Leveller as it turned towards the heart of the forest. For the first time, panic and chaos ruled in FernGully.

Crysta saw Ock and Rock cowering at the foot of the strangler fig tree. Her heart went out to Magi's two loyal friends. She hoped some day she could help them understand why Magi had left them. She was relieved to see that old Potsy was alive and huddled next to them, keeping them company.

'Crysta!' shrieked Blackbeak. 'I've moved all the young inside *Old Hi Rise*. Rose Myrtle and Granny are in there with them. The rest of us are ready to fight!'

20

THE LEVELLER

Zak knew only too well that the Leveller would flatten FernGully. But, as hard as he tried, he could not persuade the fairy folk to leave.

The Leveller was an extremely efficient machine. It could level whole sections of the forest in less time than it took dozens of machines to do the same job. When Zak had first seen it, he'd been impressed. It was built to chop, cut, saw and stack timber as it crawled along on its wide caterpillar tyres. And it could travel through any terrain at a surprisingly fast speed for its gigantic size. It was being tested out in the rainforest, and everyone who'd worked with it agreed that its performance was faultless.

Zak knew the forest didn't have a chance of surviving the Leveller. He hadn't thought when he came to work at the logging camp during his school holidays that this machine would end up killing him, for he knew that if he stayed with the fairy folk he would almost certainly die. But when he tried to tell everyone of the overwhelming odds against them, no-one would listen.

'This is our home,' said Jips. 'We'll stay and fight.'

'We will not run away!' agreed Grandfather Ash.

'But what will you fight with?' argued Zak, 'your wings?'

'No,' said Crysta quietly, 'we'll use the power of this forest. If we face the *masheen* and Hexxus together...' But her words were cut short as the ground trembled again and the sky darkened, and they all knew Hexxus was leading the Leveller straight towards them.

Inside *Old Hi Rise*, baby birds and tiny animals huddled together as the huge tree swayed and groaned. Rose Myrtle and Granny Belladonna tried to calm the baby fairies, while Silky played mother to a cluster of rose robin chicks who were hungry and squawking for food. Baby geckos, miniature frogs and tiny snakes were crowded together beside newborn echidnas and marsupial mice. Paddy looked huge compared to most of them—only young Poss and Gloss were anywhere near his size. Many of the young were already injured, and Mother Ash was busy attending to as many as she could.

'What's that noise?' whimpered Treena echidna.

'Why is the earth moving?' cried Paddy.

'It's all right. We're safe in here,' replied Rose Myrtle in her best no-nonsense voice.

'Hope she's right,' whispered Fern, stroking a frightened baby caterpillar. 'What if it's the end of the world? Where do we go from here?'

'The Elders will think of something,' replied Lily.

'But have you seen Hexxus?' said Fern. 'He's

enormous!' Lily's reply was drowned out by the battle raging outside.

The forest was fighting back, but it was a losing battle. The birds flocked together and rigged up an elaborate maze of interwoven vines. The trees interlocked their branches and formed a barricade against the Leveller. But the huge machine just ripped through the vines and cut down the trees.

The Beetle Boys arrived with their whole gang and charged at Hexxus. They flew around his head in tight circles, buzzing in and out of his ears to distract him, while the others tried to halt the massive machine.

Batty Koda joined the Beetle Boys. 'Rip snort, we're fanging on the wild side, now! Let's eliminate his master blaster!'

But Batty was no match for Hexxus—he was quickly hurled to earth, bleeping furiously.

The Leveller was now advancing towards *Old Hi Rise* at a steady pace. Zak knew the hopelessness of the situation, he knew there was nothing anyone in the forest could do to stop this killing machine. But he knew there was something *he* could do!

Without a thought for his own safety, Zak ran through a thick wall of smoke towards the machine, not seeing the machine's scissor hands snapping at him. If Batty Koda hadn't swooped in and scooped him up, he would have been sliced in two.

'Fractured figs! This is the last time I save you,' said Batty, dodging the fireballs Hexxus was blasting all around them.

But Zak didn't want to be carried to safety, he wanted to get inside the machine.

'What? Are you crazy?' shrieked Batty.

'There, above that doorway,' shouted Zak.

Batty circled the Leveller, but was sent spinning when Hexxus lashed out at the Beetle Boys and winged Batty instead. Zak was hurled from Batty's grasp and thrown against the Leveller's oily windshield. He slid down it, but before he dropped to almost certain death underneath the machine's caterpillar tyres, he managed to grab a windscreen wiper and stop his fall. He clung to the blade and pounded on the windshield, in the hope that the men driving the Leveller would see him.

The men did notice something, so they turned on the windscreen wipers for a better look. Zak suddenly found himself riding the blade. He knew he couldn't hold on for very long, especially when Hexxus circled the giant machine and began to shake it.

Then everything seemed to happen at once.

The two men inside the Leveller saw Hexxus for the first time. They screamed at the hideous, distorted face leering at them through the windscreen, dripping globs of oil. They opened the cabin door, falling over each other to get away from the nightmare creature towering above their machine, and abandoned the Leveller. They ran off into the forest, screaming.

Unable to hold on any longer, Zak started to slide down the windscreen. To his surprise, Pips suddenly appeared out of the smoke and yanked him to safety. With Pips' help, he managed to scramble inside the cabin. Gasping for breath, he summoned his last reserves of strength and crawled across the oil-spattered control panel. Slipping and sliding, he reached the huge ignition key and managed to turn it to OFF.

The Leveller immediately shuddered and stopped, its saw blades grinding to a halt just in front of *Old Hi Rise*. Hexxus froze, then in a fury of blind rage he smashed the Leveller, trying to restart it.

Zak dived out of the door as the cabin crashed around him. Once again Pips flew to his rescue, trying to cushion his fall. But Zak was heavier, and the two of them plummeted towards the ground.

'This is incredibulge!' shrieked Batty, scooping them up before they hit the ground. 'It's gravity gross-out time.'

But before they could escape, Batty was hit by a piece of flying metal. Pips and Zak were flung to safety, but Batty crash-landed. The last they saw of him was the tip of his wing poking out from under a huge chunk of twisted steel plating.

Mel the pademelon and young Paddy.

21
CRYSTA FACES HEXXUS

Crysta saw Batty fall. She flew down to where he lay under the twisted steel, but there was nothing she could do to help him.

'No!' she cried, trying to stop the tears, because there was no time for tears right now. She was in danger of being hit by the hail of flying metal that Hexxus was blowing about him as he ripped into the Leveller.

By now the clouds of thick smoke made it almost impossible to breathe. Most of the trees were down, and hundreds of forest creatures lay dead or dying. Crysta vowed she would destroy Hexxus, even if it meant her life, for without the forest she might as well be dead.

She dug into her magic pouch and took out the seed Magi Lune had given her. It glowed in her hand, and she remembered Magi Lune telling her that the love she felt for this forest would give her a strength Hexxus knew nothing about. As she held the seed, she knew she must now tap into her own hidden power.

The glowing seed reminded her of the magic she shared with all life, and as this feeling grew she felt close to Magi Lune. She could almost see her floating at her side. And with that thought, hundreds of fairies suddenly appeared and fluttered around her.

Hexxus was still charging at the Leveller in his vain attempts to start it. He stopped every now and again to suck on the exhaust pipes, and when nothing came out of them his rage increased. He was working himself into a terrible temper now that his fuel supply had evaporated. At the height of his fury he smashed the Leveller to pieces, then rose up in a gigantic column of concentrated evil and raged above what was left of the canopy.

'Together we *can* stop him,' said Crysta, as more fairies and elves rallied around her.

But none of them expected the wild whirlwind that suddenly sucked them all high into the air—Hexxus had extended an arm out of his swirling body of poisonous clouds and shredded the rest of the canopy. Then he inhaled his own angry billowing fumes. With every breath he took he created a whirlwind of destruction. He was blowing himself up to terrifying proportions, preparing for his final attack.

'You tried to stop me once before,' he screamed, scorching the trees with every harsh word. 'And now you are about to learn that I am the most powerful force in existence. Now that I've been freed, nothing can stop me from destroying until there's nothing left to destroy! Goodbye forest! Goodbye fairies!'

Crysta knew this was her last chance. So when Hexxus inhaled again, she acted. Instead of fighting against the intake of air, she streaked towards him, dodging the flying debris that was being sucked through the air.

As she flew towards Hexxus, a ray of sunlight zapped through the dark clouds and struck the seed in her outstretched hand. The seed suddenly sprouted, then before Hexxus knew what had happened she'd flown into his open mouth and disappeared. He'd swallowed both Crysta and the magic seed.

Hexxus billowed above *Old Hi Rise* coughing and spluttering as he choked on this unexpected mouthful. He roared in pain as the seed started to grow inside him. He bellowed out his anger when a vine burst out of the top of his head. He inhaled and puffed himself up, but this only accelerated the growth of the seed, and more and more vines shot out of his body.

The seed was growing at a magical rate. It was growing into a strangler fig tree.

The vines exploding out of Hexxus thickened into steely tendrils and took root. Hexxus reared up against them but they pulled him down. Roaring at the top of his voice, he dragged himself through the devastated forest, trying to break loose. But he was grounded, and there was nothing he could do about it.

The air vibrated with his fury as Hexxus battled against the power of nature. He fought and struggled with all his might, but with every contortion he bent himself into increasingly ugly shapes. He was being strangled by the tree inside him. He tried to shrink himself and wriggle free, but the vine roots had meshed together so tightly that he couldn't escape. Soon his voice was only a muffled roar.

Zak and Pips stood side by side as they watched the strangler fig grow and grow and grow, until it towered above the torn canopy. Now there was hardly any sign of Hexxus at all. Only the faintest outline of his face was frozen forever, way up in the massive tree trunk.

When the tree finally stopped growing, Zak and Pips ran towards it. Pips flew around it, looking for some sign of Crysta. Zak hunted around the newly-formed roots.

'Down here!' shouted Zak, disappearing into a hollow between the buttressed roots. Pips joined him, and they found Crysta curled up in a tight ball, carefully tucked up and protected by the root system of the tree.

'Oh Crys, please wake up,' Pips cried. He lifted her up in his arms and kissed her gently.

To his surprise, she opened her eyes and smiled up at him. He carried her out of the tree and everyone cheered when they saw her. Frogs leapt in the air, and even the serious snakes grinned.

'Is that a party I hear?' yelled Granny Belladonna, peering out of *Old Hi Rise*.

'It sure is, Granny!' shouted Pips. 'Crysta is safe, Hexxus is dead, and the Leveller has been destroyed. Everyone can come out now.'

'Oh my goodness!' cried Rose Myrtle, fluttering out of *Old Hi Rise*. 'Whatever happened to our forest?'

There was much rejoicing now that the battle was

over, and Crysta was honoured for her bravery, but it was also a sad time for everyone. Their beautiful forest was in ruins and so many lives had been lost.

Among the fallen trees and debris there were also many injured animals. Pips organised flocks of birds to lift them to safety, while Blackbeak worked with Ock and Rock to turn the soil carefully in the search for missing friends. Magi Lune and Batty were gone, and Draggs had died in the beech tree circle. Wilkea and Knot were alive, but badly injured.

Zak felt dreadful; he knew he should have warned them about the logging camp at the edge of the forest, but he'd never dreamt it could so quickly lead to this sort of destruction. Crysta sat beside him and held his hand as the last of the dark clouds blew away. She knew how he felt. His pain was her pain too.

'You risked your life for us. You belong here, Zak. You're a part of us now.'

22
THE GREENING

Once the injured had been taken care of in makeshift shelters, everyone gathered around Crysta and Zak.

'You risked your life for all of us, Crysta,' said Ash, proudly hugging his daughter.

'Magi Lune was right,' sighed Elwood, tugging his singed beard. 'We must remember the Old Powers. Knowledge must never be lost.'

'Don't forget, it was Zak who stopped the *masheen*,' said Crysta.

Jips agreed that without Zak they wouldn't have had a chance. 'We're lucky to have you with us.'

But Zak told them he couldn't stay. He told them he had to go back to his own world to make sure no-one ever tried to destroy their rainforest again.

Crysta pointed to the new strangler fig tree and they watched flocks of noisy parrots and other birds move into the tree and build new nests. They laughed at Queenie flapping around *Old Hi Rise*. She was moving her nest up a few branches away from Blackbeak's perch.

'You're going to missss the food he dropsss,' said Greeney, who was curled up around his favourite branch, nursing his wounded tail.

'Go photosynth yourself,' squawked Queenie, cleaning out her nest. 'At least it will be more peaceful without that loud-beak hanging over me.'

'FernGully will be back to normal faster than we think,' said Crysta, smiling.

Pips flew down beside them. When he found out Zak was leaving, he was genuinely sorry. He'd seen first-hand how Zak had risked his life for them all. Zak had proved himself to be a true friend. Zak had also made Pips realise how much he loved Crysta, so much so that now he wanted to learn and practise the Old Powers too.

Pips stepped forward and hugged Zak. 'We're going to miss you. You might be a human, but you're a good one.'

'Thanks,' laughed Zak, touched by Pips' open display of friendship. 'Keep the stereo, dude. It's yours, now.'

'Thanks, *dood*,' Pips said, grinning.

Blackbeak flapped overhead and called to Crysta.

'Honey-berry, I've just seen two more humans in Sleepy Hollow and they're wandering around in circles.'

'Ralph and Tony,' said Zak, remembering the two men who'd been driving the Leveller. 'I'll have to find them.'

Blackbeak offered him a lift, and Crysta said she'd fly as far as Sleepy Hollow with them. Everyone waved goodbye to Zak, saying they hoped he'd come back one day.

When they flew into Sleepy Hollow, Crysta was relieved to see that Little Hoop was still standing. Some of its branches were missing, but it was bristling with life. It hadn't grown into the tallest tree, and it didn't look very strong, but it was certainly one of the happiest-looking trees in the forest. Stoneface, who was covered in leaves and dirt, looked happy, too.

Blackbeak showed them where the two men were stumbling around Sleepy Hollow. Watching them, Crysta knew it was time for Zak to join his own kind.

'They aren't so bad,' said Zak. 'They just don't understand why this forest is so special.'

'They'll learn,' said Crysta. 'But not even the Old Powers permit us to tamper with free will. Everyone can learn to see things differently, but only when they want to.'

'I wish I was as positive as you,' he said, full of admiration.

'Don't forget the magic we share,' said Crysta, handing him a seed from her pouch. 'And remember, the magic grows when it's shared. Remember, Zak; remember everything.'

Zak closed his fist around the seed, and he kissed her for the last time. It was a kiss of love and friendship and there were tears in his eyes as he walked away.

Crysta raised her arm and softly chanted,
What was done, now undo,
return you to the form that's true.

With every step Zak took, he grew taller. Ralph and Tony were amazed and delighted to see him, and were only too happy to follow him out of Sleepy Hollow.

As they walked through what was left of the forest, Zak discovered that the tiny things he'd noticed before were now blurred and many of them disappeared from sight altogether. They passed *Old Hi Rise*, but all he could see were flocks of birds sitting in the branches. He couldn't see the fairies and elves all around him, but he could feel their presence.

He stepped over a twisted chunk of metal and stared at the wing tip sticking out from under it. He lifted up the metal plate and there in a dug-out burrow, lay Batty Koda!

He picked Batty up and held him gently in his hands. How small he looked now!

'Aargghh!' shrieked Batty, suddenly opening his eyes and staring at Zak. 'I've been shrunk!'

'No you haven't,' said Zak. 'I've grown. Are you okay?'

'I guess so . . .' muttered Batty, shaking his head and looking around him.

'Are you sure?'

'I'm positive,' grinned Batty.

Zak opened his hands and Batty flew away.

'What happened?' Ralph asked, standing dazed amid the remains of the Leveller and staring up at the torn canopy.

Zak didn't know what to say as he looked at the ravaged forest, so he took the seed Crysta had given him and planted it. As he walked away he didn't look back, for he'd started the long journey back to his own world.

The sun shone down on the seed and it sprouted,

and as the plant grew, a few lone trees started to sing. Batty flapped back onto *Old Hi Rise*, much to the delight of Crysta and the fairy folk, who were overjoyed to see him alive and well. Then everyone began to sing, as the song of the trees touched their hearts. The fairies formed a dazzling spiral, and danced in time to the music, as the heart of the forest burst into life.

Crysta emerged from the spiral of fairies, and streaked towards the sky. She twisted and turned and dived to the forest floor in a stunning display of aerobatics. She flew like she'd never flown before. The singing grew louder, the greenery spread, and Crysta glowed with happiness.

Pips joined her, and they danced in the sunshine.

'Is it time for the party?' shouted Granny Belladonna, poking her head out of *Old Hi Rise*.

'Yes,' shouted the fairy folk, 'it's time to celebrate the greening.'

'Groovacious!' bleeped Batty, dropping off his branch and joining the fairies in their celebration dance.